Martini Afternoons

Beverly Fortenberry

Library of Congress Control Number:		2017913037
ISBN:	Hardcover	978-1-5434-4609-8
	Softcover	978-1-5434-4610-4
	eBook	978-1-5434-4611-1

Print information available on the last page.

Rev. date: 09/05/2017

To order additional copies of this book, contact:
Xlibris
1-888-795-4274
www.Xlibris.com
Orders@Xlibris.com
766180

Martini Afternoons

Acknowledgements

My thanks goes out to many people and one very special place. Poydras Home, where this book was written, was founded in 1817 as a place where widows and orphans could find a safe haven. As time progressed, it evolved into what it is today; a retirement community for men and women. It has more than three acres of beautiful grounds filled with leafy trees and lovely flowers. It provided me with inspiration both because of its physical environment, but also because of its warm and helpful administrators and staff.

The residents of Poydras Home are a fascinating group of people. As I got to know them better I learned that there were those who had been active in congressional affairs, others who had been involved in running some of the larger local businesses. In addition there are residents who had practiced medicine or held commands in the military during World War II.

If I were to list all those who supplied me with ideas or experiences that found their way into this book, I would have to list every resident because they all helped shape this book.

Finally a special thanks to Joni Fisher, author of the Compass Crime Series, for her helpful literary advice.

Chapter 1

It was autumn in Bexley, Indiana. The leaves on the maple trees proliferating its streets glowed red and gold against a brilliant blue sky. The small town located between Terre Haute and Bloomington was an ideal location for the families of commuters to both towns. Yes, Bexley had become the town of choice for those working in these nearby cities.

Over the past few years, the houses along Maple Drive in Bexley had under gone major transformations. Gone were all the bungalows that had been built during the 1940s and 1950s. Some had been torn down and replaced with stately colonials or impressive minimansions; others had been renovated, adding second stories, porches, gazebos, and patios. All this gentrification made number 610 stand out. Henry and Edith Harris had bought the house for $3,100 in 1939. It was a popular style back then, but times and tastes had changed.

Number 610's clapboard shingles had faded to a pale gray and the window frames to a dull green. The front yard had grass that was uneven, as if it had been cut with a Weed Wacker rather than a lawn mower. Its bushes, which had been planted many years ago, had grown tall and rangy along the sides of the lot. All in all, it looked forlorn and neglected; that is until you looked at the windows, which were bright and shiny. At least some care was being taken.

Henry Harris had passed away several years ago. He had been a contractor, responsible for erecting bridges and dams all over the world. Since most of his work was in fairly remote places, Henry's wife, Edith, had stayed at home. Henry came home every three months or so, and each time, they would celebrate his return by having a few martinis as he shared his latest experiences with Edith. Each time he returned, it was like they were having a second honeymoon. Edith missed Henry and those martini afternoons very much. But since she lived alone now, sipping a martini by herself didn't seem right. She needed someone with whom she could share the martini ritual she had once shared with Henry.

Since they had had no children, and there were no close relatives, Edith now lived alone in the cottage. She kept the interior spotless, but since she had had a stroke two years ago, her legs were not too stable, which made outside maintenance beyond her ability. She had tried hiring yardmen, but they didn't always show up and sometimes charged so much she just couldn't afford it. She was, after all, on a strict budget. She finally gave up on the yard, using her Weed Wacker to try and level the grass out when it got too long.

Most of Edith's neighbors were young. The wives either worked or seemed to jog and go to yoga classes. Edith had politely turned down requests for her to sit with their toddlers. She didn't want to become an auxiliary grandparent, chasing after wee ones all day long. She was sure that once she took on that role, she would become the neighborhood sitter—a role she didn't want.

Edith didn't mind living alone, she always found something to do in her house. What she did miss was having someone to talk to—maybe not every day, but someone to carry on a conversation with once in a while. A conversation about almost anything would be nice from time to time. She started thinking about a way to have someone in once or twice a month for a little social hour, or at least that was what she called it. The thing was coming up with who she could invite and what they would talk about.

Idly, she glanced down at the worn carpet in her den. *I wish I could replace this old carpet*, she thought. And then, the idea hit her. She could invite a carpet salesperson in to show her rug samples. While she was looking at the samples, she could serve some cocktails and steer the conversation around to other topics in addition to carpets. Since she was just looking at the samples at this point, she wouldn't have to commit to anything, she could tell the person she would have to think about their product and get back to them. No commitment, but perhaps a pleasant afternoon.

The ad for Classic Carpets sounded very nice. They said they would come to your home with samples for you to review. *Just the ticket!* she thought. And so Edith's foray into "sample social hours" began.

"Hello? Classic Carpets? This is Mrs. Edith Harris calling. I am thinking of redoing some carpeting and would like a salesperson to come to my home and show me some samples. I'm thinking of some shade of green wool. When would you have someone available? Next Wednesday at two o'clock would be fine. The address is 610 Maple Drive. Yes, our street has had a lot of renovation. I am just a shade tardy in starting mine. Whom shall I expect on Wednesday? John Wilklow, fine. Thank you."

Edith looked into the mirror on the wall over the sofa. Ruefully she considered herself. In her midsixties, she still was a pixie-like woman with silver streaking through her soft brown hair. She had grown a bit plump, but the liveliness of her hazel eyes and the smoothness of her skin helped to make her look younger than her years.

Lemon sprigs on the coffee table, ice in the ice bucket, martini glasses in the fridge and the martini fixings in the pitcher. She was a bit nervous—what if he didn't like martinis? Well, she could just switch him to something else. She sat in the club chair in her den with its ceiling-to-floor bookcases, each filled with a lifetime of memorabilia. She looked around, noting pictures of the many places Henry had been. Her eyes slowed to enjoy some of the bits and pieces he had collected from his stops around the globe. How nice and comforting it all looked. *Oh dear, there was the doorbell!*

"Mr. Wilklow? Please do come in, young man. I am so glad you could come to show me some samples of carpet that may just fit my needs. As I explained when I called, it seems the rest of the street has already been busy with their updating. I am a bit tardy with my plans. I thought I would, you know, do one thing at a time.

"What is your first name? Oh, it is John. I feel so formal calling you Mr. Wilklow. If you don't mind, I will call you John, then. Please sit here by the coffee table and put your samples on the floor so I can look at them as we talk. I have prepared my afternoon martini, and it would be such a pleasure if you would join me.

"Oh! These colors are quite lovely. Tell me about their wool content. I want a sturdy wool that will hold up. John, before we start, I seem to have emptied my glass. Would you be so kind as to refill it for me? Oh, and please make one for yourself. I hate to drink alone. I will just look through your samples as you top me up and prepare one for yourself.

"I see you found everything ready in the fridge. Thank you for refilling my glass. I know, I know, but having a few martinis in the afternoon won't kill me. At my age, I don't think it will do much more damage than I have already inflicted upon my body. I look at it as medication that is both healthful and therapeutic."

John sat down across the coffee table from Edith and said, "Well, ma'am, this is the first time I have been offered something like a martini as I discuss carpeting with a client. Usually the most I get is a cup of coffee. However, if you insist, I guess I can have a martini with you. Here, I'll refill your glass for you. As I do so, please look over the carpet choices in the sample packet. I can see a soft forest green in this room and hall. Be right back."

"Thank you, John," Edith said as she took a fresh glass from the young man. Umm, it is nice and cold, just as I like it. You look so young. How long have you worked for Classic Carpet?"

"Oh, I'm not so young. Pushing thirty this November. I have been with Classic going on four years. Now this wool sample is in the color I have suggested, and at thirty dollars a yard, quite a good buy. What do you think, Mrs. Harris?"

"Let me look at it and review some of the other colors. Before you started with Classic Carpets, what did you do? Were you in college or the military? My late husband was in the Air Force before he became a contractor. What about you?"

"Well, after I graduated from high school, I didn't know what I wanted to do, so I went into the Marines, spent time in Afghanistan and other areas over there. Then when I got discharged, I came home and got this job with Classic. I would like to go back to school, but with a wife and new baby, I don't know if I can swing it."

"My husband used to say, sometimes you have to make your opportunities. What's that old cliché? 'Seize the day.' There are night classes at the community college. Have you thought about going there?"

"I have thought about it, but frankly, I am afraid if I start, I may find my time too stretched. This job isn't nine-to-five. Sometimes I have to work evenings and even weekends.

"John, would you replenish our glasses? We both seem to need a refill. I rather like this light shade of green."

"Sure, Mrs. Harris, I will refill your glass. I really have to get going pretty soon. This certainly has been the nicest meeting I have ever had. I have another stop to make, and if I have one more martini, I may not be able to make it. Have you made up your mind on which carpet you want?"

"Oh, John, I am so sorry you have to leave, but I know business comes first. Tell you what. If you have some small samples you can leave with me I will look them over and get back to you. Would that be all right?"

"Sure, we leave small samples with clients all the time. When should I call for your decision?"

"Let me get back to you. It may be a few days. I do hope that is not going to be a problem, John."

"Certainly not. I will look forward to hearing from you. Thank you for the drinks and for your interest in our product."

"Why, thank you, John. You have been most gracious and helpful. Let me walk you to the door."

Edith saw the carpet salesman out. Slowly she walked into her den, carrying the green wool samples. She opened a cupboard next to the fireplace and placed the samples inside. With a satisfied smile on her face, she walked into the kitchen to clean up the martini glasses. The little experiment had gone rather well. She had passed a pleasant time with John, the carpet man, and enjoyed having a companion with whom to share her afternoon martinis. Edith considered what she could try next. Perhaps she could find someone who could show her some kitchen tile or granite countertops. She would look into this tomorrow.

Several months had passed since Edith had started her sample social hours. Her cupboard now contained, in addition to the rug samples, paint chips for her bedroom and dining room, small pieces of granite for the kitchen counters, samples of vinyl tile for the kitchen floor, a sample of wood flooring in oak, brochures for a step-in bathtub, a slate patio, paint colors for the cottage and several window treatments. All in all, she had found these little social hours most pleasant. And when they called to see what her decisions were, she just put them off by saying she was not ready to make a commitment. After a while, they stopped calling.

Bright sunshine flooded her kitchen as Edith had her morning coffee and looked over her mail. As usual, it was mostly advertising flyers and requests for donations to some cause or another. At the bottom of the stack was a letter. Personal mail was a rarity for Edith. She looked at the return address. Well for heaven's sake, it was from her old school friend, Estella! What a treat to get a letter from her.

"Dear Edi," the letter began. Back in school, she had been called Edi, and her friend Estella had been called Elli. Edi and Elli had been the closest of friends. But time and careers had led to distant locations and had prevented them from seeing each other. As Edith read on, she learned that Elli's husband, Richard, had passed away a year ago. Elli was on her own and wanted to come and see Edi. Oh, that would be just wonderful!

Back when both were gay young things, they used to feel very sophisticated sitting in a cocktail lounge sipping martinis and giggling over each other's current boyfriend. Edith looked up and realized she wouldn't need to host any more sample social hours. She and Elli could have their own martini afternoons! That is, if Elli still drank martinis. It was going to be such fun, having Elli with her. She immediately wrote a letter to Elli saying how thrilled she would be to have her come and stay for as long as she could. Once the letter was posted, she embarked on a thorough cleaning of the guest bedroom.

* * *

"Hello?" The phone rang, and Edith had to hurry to get it. "Oh my goodness, Elli! Did you get my letter? Yes, yes, of course I want you to come and stay as long as you can. It will almost be like being back in school. We have so many years to catch up on with each other. I have already got your room ready. When can you get here? No, I don't have a car. You will have to get a taxi. It is only a few miles. Oh, I am so looking forward to seeing you. All right, see you on Saturday!"

* * *

Elli was a nickname from school days. Most people knew her as Estella, which was her given name. She sat dejectedly on the edge of her bed in her drab and dingy one-room apartment. All her worldly goods were in that room. Two suitcases, a small china vase that had belonged to her mother, and her clothes, all rather old and worn. She certainly didn't look or feel like the eager and energetic young woman who had left school with Edith all those years ago. Her hair was still a light auburn but with streaks of silver-gray. And her figure was still slender, but time and care added fine lines and hollows to her face. She wondered how she would look to her old friend.

For Estella, the years had had more downs than ups. She had been swept off her feet by the charming and handsome young man she met on her vacation in San Francisco. Richard Collier had wined and dined her and told her of the exciting future he envisioned for them. She was dazzled by his looks and his plans for the both of them. Impulsively, she agreed to marry him. It wasn't long before she realized he was a charming dreamer who was looking for his ship to come in. He took one job after another, but never could find something he either liked or was good at. He kept saying his chance was just around the corner, but it never was. She managed to save a bit, but the bills were always a worry. When he died of a heart attack, she had had to sell their house to pay the bills that he owed. He had cancelled the life insurance to get money for another of his schemes. So with no insurance, she had only the money she had squirreled away. It came to a pitiful amount. Estella sighed and thought she was now like Blanche DuBois in *A Streetcar Named Desire*, dependent on the kindness of others. In this case, the kindness of Edi.

With a sigh, Estella completed her packing and took a cab, squandering a little of her savings, as there were no buses from her neighborhood to the airport. Once there, she sat in the airport lounge waiting for her flight to be called. If she hadn't had to sell their car, she would have driven, saving the cost of the flight, but such was not the case. Once her flight was called and she had settled into her coach seat, she leaned back and began to wonder how the years had been for her old friend Edith.

* * *

As the taxi pulled up to Edith's cottage, Estella took a deep breath. She would tell Edi the truth and hope she was willing to take her in as a roommate, willing to do whatever she could to pay for her keep. Resolutely, she got out of the taxi and walked to the front door.

"Elli! Oh, it's so good to see you. You haven't aged a bit. Look at you, hair still that lovely auburn, and you are still so slim and trim! Oh, what fun we are going to have. I hope you can stay long enough for us to catch up on all the years we missed. Let's get your bags in your room, and then we can sit down and have a nice long chat. This is like old times," she said gaily.

With Edith leading the way, they managed to carry Estella's bags to the spare bedroom. All the while, Edith kept chattering on about how excited she was to have her friend come to stay with her. "I certainly hope you plan to stay a long time. We have years to relive," she said.

Ruefully, Estella replied, "Oh, I am sure we will have plenty of time, dear Edi. And I have quite a bit to share with you." With that, Estella sat down on the edge of the bed and patted the quilt next to her and asked Edith to sit down.

"I need to bare my soul right away, old friend. The truth is, I am in a dreadful financial situation, and I was hoping I might impose on your generous nature and our old friendship and that you might let me live with you. Of course, I will help with the housework and yard and anything else I can to pay for my living here." With that, Estella bowed her head and cupped her hands over her eyes as the tears slowly ran through her fingers.

Edith sat next to her old friend and stared sadly at her. Slowly, she put her arm around her friend's shoulders and gently rubbed her forehead against Estella's hair. "Of course, you can stay with me. We are like sisters, and that is what sisters do—they take care of each other. What we need to do now is go down to the kitchen and fix ourselves some tea, and you can tell me what happened to put you in such a fix."

Estella hugged Edith and thanked her. Together, arm in arm, they made their way to the kitchen. Once comfortably settled in chairs at the table with cups of tea, Edith repeated her query. "What happened?"

With a sigh, Estella began her sad story. She told Edith how Richard was always trying one get-rich-quick scheme after another. He didn't like working for someone, having to follow their rules and live from paycheck to paycheck. He wanted to make a lot of money and be his own boss. Only every scheme he tried failed, and they often moved just ahead of Richard's creditors. Estella hadn't told anyone about their difficulties because she was ashamed. Besides, how do you explain your troubles in a note or a Christmas card?

Estella tried to save money whenever she could. The funny thing was, everyone really liked Richard. He was charming, good-looking, and could talk anyone into anything when he wanted to. He was sure he would hit the jackpot with the next venture. Unfortunately, he never did. He died of a heart attack at one of his investor meetings, leaving Estella to clean up the financial debris he left. By the time she had paid their debts by selling their house and emptying what little they had in the bank, she was left with the little bit she had saved.

"I have heard enough. Of course, you can stay here. I wouldn't want it any other way. I am sure if I had ended up in your boat, you would have taken me in. I mean, after all, we are like sisters, aren't we? We should be thankful we have each other. By the way, do you still like martinis? I hope so because it is just about time for my afternoon martini."

Estella smiled gratefully at Edith and said, "I adore martinis. They still make me feel gay and young. I haven't had the occasion to drink many in the last few years."

Edith flushed a bit as she said, "Well, it has been a bit lonely since Henry died. I didn't want to be the neighborhood babysitter, and there aren't any other older people living here. So what I have done to have a little social life has been to invite in salespeople to show me rug samples, paint samples, patio tiles, and every other home improvement I could think of. I would call, and they would come in to show me product samples. While they were here, I would get them to share a martini or two with me as we discussed their products. I never ordered anything, but it gave me a little outlet." After saying this, she took Estella into the den and showed her all the samples she had acquired.

Estella giggled. "Oh, Edi, how clever you have been. Why, if we were to go on with your little sample social hours, we could do—oh, let me think—we could invite contractors to add a second floor or a gazebo and a patio or . . . Why, for heaven's sake! We could keep this going for ages. What fun!"

Edith handed Estella a notebook and suggested they make a list of home improvements they could do to add spice to their martini afternoons. Like two girls in school working on a class project, they spent the afternoon strategizing their future.

The next day, after breakfast, they took a walk down Maple Drive. Edi pointed out the houses that had been renovated and of course pointed out the minimansions that had replaced so many of the old homes. Signs for the different contractors who were currently working on the homes still being rebuilt were easy to spot along the way. Elli opened a notebook she was carrying and stopped to write down the names and phone numbers on their signs.

"Edi, these are the contractors we can call to look at your home. We just have to decide what kind of renovations you want to make."

"What renovations *we* want to make. After all, it is our home now. I am just so happy that we are going to be living together. So it is our home, and we are going to have such pleasant times." As she said this, Edi smiled fondly at Elli and reached up to put her arm around her friend. She gave her a pat and then said in a more businesslike manner, "We will need to decide what we want done to the house so we will be prepared to discuss our plans with each contractor. Should we ask for the same plan from each of them?"

"I think we could have some variety," said Elli. Perhaps we could divide up the list of contractors and with one list, discuss renovating and with the other, a complete redo. What do you think?"

"Oh, I don't know. I think we should ask for different forms of renovation from each of them. Maybe variations on adding a second story, adding rooms to the back of the house along with a patio and gazebo. What do you think?"

"Sounds like a more practical approach. Right now, we need to look through some magazines to get some ideas of what we might want. Then we can make up a call list. I'm getting excited. This is going to be a real adventure!"

The two copied down the names and phone numbers of the contractors as they made their way down the street. By the time they had walked to the end of Maple Drive where it entered a small park, they had completed their list of builders, and they turned to make their way home.

Chapter 2

Stan Baxter looked once again at the telephone message slip in his hand. Yep, the address was 610 Maple Drive. The message said they wanted to talk about doing some renovation. Stan—owner of Baxter Construction, a local company with a thirty-five-year reputation—considered the small clapboard cottage once more. To him, the cottage didn't need renovating. It needed to be torn down and replaced with a totally new home. As he rang the doorbell, he thought about what he could say that might talk them into replacing their cottage.

The door opened, and Stan looked down on a petite woman with gray-streaked auburn hair who was dressed in a pale pink sweater and slacks. She smiled up at him and said, "Hello, may I help you?"

"I certainly hope so. I'm Stan Baxter of Baxter Construction. Someone called and asked me to come to talk about doing some renovation."

"Oh yes. We did call you. Thank you so much for coming. You are right on time, Mr. Baxter. Edi and I are interested in what you can do for us." As she said this, Elli led Stan into the living room.

"It is my pleasure to meet with you ladies. Will anyone else be joining us for this meeting? Your husbands, for instance?"

"Elli smiled demurely and answered, "We are both widows, Mr. Baxter. We know our little home stands out on this street with all the changes our neighbors have made. That is why we want to try to bring our place a little more up to date." Saying this, she led Stan to the couch and patted the seat next to where she started to sit.

Stan thought that she was certainly an attractive woman, and he wondered how close to his age she was. His wife had passed away two years ago, and even though he wasn't looking to remarry, it was nice to be with such a charming woman.

"Elli, won't you introduce us?" Edi had walked in from the kitchen. She was carrying a sheaf of pictures that she placed on the coffee table in front of Stan.

"Edi, this is Mr. Baxter of Baxter Construction. He is here to talk with us about the renovation we are thinking of doing. May we call you Stan rather than Mr. Baxter?"

"Why, sure, and what may I call you two charming ladies?"

"I am Edi, and the lady sitting next to you is Elli. We share this cottage. We know that the whole neighborhood has gone through lots of changes, and we are late getting our plans started. But we love this place and are so comfortable that we hated to get involved with all the mess that will come from renovating."

With that she spread out the pictures she had placed on the table, explaining that these were examples of what they had in mind. "As you can see from these pictures, we are considering expanding our living room out in the back to add a sun room and a covered porch— something like what you see in this picture."

Stan looked at the picture she handed him. It showed a living area that flowed into a garden room and ended with French doors leading into an outside covered patio. The renovation would enlarge the back of the cottage by about 1,200 to 1,300 square feet. He thought that they would be better off just tearing down the old cottage and starting over. However, wanting to start off on the right foot, he decided to go slow and ask some questions to hear why they wanted to make this type of change.

"I would like to get a better understanding of what your overall goal is. For example, is this all you want to do, or are you planning further changes in the future? If you have other changes you want to make, getting all of them in the right order at the beginning would be a good idea."

Edi nodded and said, "Before we begin to discuss our plans, perhaps you might like to join us for a little afternoon refreshment?"

"Certainly. I would be pleased to join you as we discuss your overall plans and goals. It is just the time of day I usually like to take a break and have a little something."

Edi clapped her hands. "A man after our own thoughts," she exclaimed. As she settled back into her club chair, Elli quietly walked into the kitchen. She was back in a few moments with a small trolley on which was placed martini glasses, a frosted pitcher, two small bowls with olives and lemon sprigs, and some napkins. As she poured, she said, "We are so glad you are willing to join us for our afternoon ritual. We always have a martini or two in the afternoon. Holding a glass up, she asked Stan if he wanted olives or lemon sprigs in his martini.

Stan was taken aback. He hadn't expected this. He was thinking they would offer him some lemonade or maybe tea or coffee, but certainly not martinis. Reminding himself that he wanted to work them around to demolishing the old cottage and building a new home, he knew he had to make a good impression. He smiled, and leaning forward, he said, "Why, ladies, I would be delighted to join you."

"Oh good, Stan. Elli, please do the honors, dear."

Elli filled their glasses, and after asking Stan if he preferred olives or lemon twists, she handed round their drinks. She sat down next to Stan and raised her glass. Glancing at Edi, she made a toast, saying, "May we find this the first of many worthwhile meetings."

As they drank their martinis, Stan asked, "What are your long-term goals for the house? Knowing this will help me to know how I might be of most help to you. After all, if you are thinking of adding a second level or expanding the cottage by adding rooms to one side or the other, it will make a difference in how I would approach the rebuilding and, of course, the costs to you."

"That certainly makes good sense, Stan. Our goal is to modernize our home, bringing it up to date. We want it to blend in with the rest of the neighborhood, but we don't want to lose the old-fashioned charm of our cottage. If we expand the back room and see how it looks, then we can consider what else we might want to do. Isn't that right, Elli?"

"Yes, that is what we talked about," said Elli. "It is easier to consider doing one thing at a time, we can get our minds around making a change that way. I suppose over time, we will end up making several additions or changes, all in keeping with enhancing our cottage."

Stan smiled and handed his glass over to Elli who promptly refilled it. He hadn't asked, but since she was already handing it back filled, he had no choice but to accept it and thank her. "Let me see if I have got this right. You want to keep the cottage and do renovations to modernize it, yet keep the cottage pretty much as is. Am I right?"

"Well, that is our initial thought. Of course, we are open to suggestions. Perhaps you might like to offer your thoughts? Just remember, we are not interested in replicating the houses that have been built so far along Maple Drive. We think our cottage has character and stands out. I don't want to look like every other house along the way."

"Well, ladies, if you want to keep the cottage feel yet make it have a more up-to-date look, we can do that. We can add the sunroom and patio that you have envisioned. We can extend the far side where the garage is and maybe add a second level and cover the entire house in a Cape Cod exterior. It would be distinctive and certainly different from every other home on Maple Drive." He paused to see what impact his words had made.

"Oh my," Edi breathed out. "That sounds absolutely lovely, doesn't it, Elli?" Elli nodded slowly. Then she added, "That sounds like it would take loads of time and a great deal of money. And all the mess it would make!"

The martini trolley was empty. Mr. Baxter was busy making notes on his pad. Edi looked at Elli and made a tiny nod. Elli rose, and taking hold of the trolley cart, she said, "I will just roll this out to the kitchen. Perhaps Edi can show you the rest of our house, and when you get back, we can decide what our next step is."

Edi and Stan left the den for the hallway. As they walked, Stan talked about the speed with which his team worked and the manner in which they were able to take the mess out of renovating.

When they came back from their tour, Elli was once again seated on the couch. Again, Stan was taken with her and wondered if it was the martinis that made her seem even more attractive.

"Mr. Baxter, this has been a good meeting. What is the next step?" Edi paused for his reply.

"What I would like to do is make a preliminary sketch of what this cottage could look like with the changes I have in mind. I could come back in a week or so to show this to you and get your reactions. Would that work for you?"

"Yes, that would be fine, although I am a little concerned about cost. Please remember, we are both widows with rather modest incomes."

With this, Edi rose and offered to walk Stan to the door, He glanced back at Elli and gave her a warm smile as he followed Edi.

* * *

"That went rather well. You know, I do think if you had batted your eyelashes at him a bit more, we might be able to get the whole house done for nothing! He seemed quite taken with you, Elli."

"Why ever would you say that?" Elli said, smiling across at Edi as they sat in the den. They had cleaned up the drinks trolley and were ready to discuss how the meeting with Mr. Baxter had gone. They had chosen him because he had done a number of the better-looking renovations on their street. They thought they should choose a solid, successful contractor, and if this went well, they could move on to the others. They even planned to invite a contractor or two who hadn't worked on the street, thinking they might be eager to get their foot in the door of the gentrification of Maple Drive.

"I liked his idea of turning this into a Cape Cod house. After all, there isn't another home like that on our street. I can almost see it a soft gray with white window frames and shutters," Elli said with a sigh.

"Now, Elli, don't get carried away with that notion. Remember, we aren't really going to do any renovating. If you want to dream about it, that is fine, but unless we win the lottery or, as I said before, you entice Mr. Baxter to marry you, we are only doing this to have some company during our afternoon social hour."

"I know, Edi, I know we aren't going to do any renovating, but it is kind of fun to dream about how it could look. When do you think he will call us back to set up a second meeting?"

"He did say he would get back to us in a week or so. I am sure he will call in a few days. I am thinking we might offer him some of my canapes to go with the drinks to sort of increase the social aspect of our discussion. What do you think, Elli?"

"Aren't you the clever one! Buttering him up with food certainly will make our next meeting more relaxed, like a real social hour."

* * *

It hadn't been a week before they heard from Stan Baxter. He said he wanted to set a date for their next meeting. He had done the sketches and was eager to get their reactions to his ideas. Edi set a date for one afternoon in the next week. While both ladies were looking forward to seeing Stan again, they were also busy setting up plans for the next contractor they were going to call. Since they were not sure how much the contractors talked about future business with each other, they had decided to call one of the contractors who had not done any work on Maple Drive. They figured such a firm might be very interested in vying for their business. So their next call was to the Tennetti Brothers. This was a smaller company with most of their expertise in home repairs and additions. When Edi called them to see if they were willing to come and discuss their home remodeling, Joe Tennetti said they would be delighted to meet. So a date was set several weeks away so as not to conflict with their planned Baxter meeting.

"We have to be careful we don't get these contractors mixed up or have them coming and going at the same time," said Edi.

"Wouldn't it be dreadful if Mr. Baxter was walking down our sidewalk just as the Tennetti Brothers were coming up it?" Elli said, laughing. Then she added in a more serious tone, "This wouldn't be very funny at all. It would ruin both our social hours and our future credibility."

"You are right. After we see Mr. Baxter again and meet with the Tennetti Brothers, let's pause for a while. After all, there is no reason to rush. We haven't set any deadlines. This is for our social pleasure, right, Edi?"

"Absolutely," Edi said, nodding.

In the meantime, Stan Baxter had spent a feverish week drawing up preliminary plans for the Cape Cod renovation. He wanted to impress the ladies with both his design as well as his efficiency. In addition, he was eager to see Elli again.

Chapter 3

Looking out the window, Edi commented, "It is beginning to look and feel like winter is coming. The trees are losing what is left of their leaves. I think it is almost cold enough to see frost in the early morning."

"And here we are talking about putting in a sun room and a patio. Mr. Baxter must think we are a couple of silly old women," Elli said, laughing.

Just then, the phone rang. Edi answered and found herself speaking to Stan Baxter. She arched her eyebrows and, looking at Elli, said, "Why hello, Mr. Baxter. How nice to hear from you. You are ready to show us your sketches along with recommendations for the improvements you think we can do? Yes, next week Wednesday at two o'clock would be fine. See you then!"

As Edi put the phone down, she remarked, "He certainly seems enthusiastic about coming to see us again. Hmm, maybe he wants to have you bat your eyes at him again."

"Oh, for heaven's sake, Edi, he just wants our business. He is a very nice man, so don't blow this out of proportion. And for your information, I have not been batting my eyes at him," Elli replied hotly.

Both ladies smiled and hugged each other. They agreed that having these contractors in for a pleasant social hour was not worth hurting their friendship. And so a truce was called, and they went back to planning their upcoming meeting in two weeks with the Tennetti Brothers. They knew this company had not worked on any of the renovations on their street and probably would want to do a job that would get their name on Maple Drive. Since they did more home repair work, Edi had suggested they ask them to talk about how they would go about replacing the current front windows on the cottage with two bay windows and a new front door with a covered porch. Elli had always loved bay windows, and when Edi suggested them, she jumped at the idea.

* * *

Stan Baxter looked in his rearview mirror to see if his hair was smoothed down. He was a bit nervous about the meeting with Edi and Elli. He wanted them to like his renovation sketches, but even more, he wanted Elli to like him enough to perhaps go to dinner with him. His main concern was how to accomplish this without alienating Edi. He got out of his car and straightened his jacket and tie as he walked to the door.

"Hello, Mr. Baxter. How nice to see you again. We are looking forward to your recommendations," Edi said, smiling at him as she led the way into the den where Elli was already seated on the couch. Stan sat in the club chair across from both women. He opened his briefcase and took out the sketches he had made. There were four of them, each one revealing one aspect of his overall design. He also took out a notebook so he could jot down any issues that arose as he described the renovation he had in mind. He glanced at Elli and gave her a warm smile.

"I have prepared a series of sketches to show you each stage of the overall design. We can consider each aspect of the rebuilding as a step moving toward this," he said as, with a flourish, he revealed his final sketch of their cottage as it would look when he had renovated it as a Cape Cod with dove-gray cedar shingles, white window frames, and a red door.

"It is absolutely lovely, Stan," Elli gushed. "It is just what I dreamed of but this is way more than we had in mind or that we can afford."

"I know it is a bit overwhelming, ladies, when you look at this final sketch. But please allow me to explain you are viewing the end of a series of smaller renovations that I am proposing over time. I wanted you to see what we would end up with in a four-phased rebuilding plan. This is the end goal. Now let me take you through each stage of the plan. For each stage, I can give you a cost estimate, and we can take our time making each change."

Stan stopped and looked over at Elli. She was as pretty as he remembered. He thought how pleasant it would be to come here every day to check on the progress of the work his team would be doing. He had pared his costs down to the bone just to get a chance to see Elli all the time.

Edi gave Elli a nod and told Stan that it was time for their afternoon refreshment ritual. "As Elli brings in our martinis, we can look at and discuss the four stages of your plan, Stan."

Stan had expected this. He smiled as he watched Elli walk into the kitchen. "Fine, I am looking forward to going over each stage with you both. And I want to assure you I am aware of your concern over costs and the mess that can come when some contractors who aren't truly professional work on this type of a project."

Elli came back with the trolley and gave Stan a warm smile as she poured the martinis. She handed round the drinks and gracefully sat down on the couch next to Edi. Edi rose and took a tray of the canapes she had prepared from the bottom of the trolley. "I thought we might want a little 'food for thought,'" she said laughing as she put the tray on the coffee table between them.

"This is a real treat," Stan said as he balanced his glass and a canape next to the Cape Cod sketch. "I have a series of sketches for you to look at. Each sketch reveals one stage of the overall restoration. Please bear in mind that these stages can take place over any time period you want to set. I don't see time as much of a priority as the completion of each part of our final plan."

Stan paused and looked at first Edi and then Elli. He was trying to gauge their degree of acceptance of his words. Neither woman said anything, although Elli gave him a warm smile. Encouraged by her positive demeanor, he picked up the first of the set of sketches he had prepared.

"As you can see in this sketch, I have included your original idea for a sunroom and patio at the back of the living room. This can be done in about ninety days with minimal disruption to your home. The cost will depend on whether this is all we do or if it is part of a larger project. Before either woman said anything, he continued. "Let's look at the second sketch showing the next stage." He laid out a sketch showing the elimination of the garage and the addition of that space to the den with a barge board wall and beams across the ceiling. "Now at this stage, we have eliminated the old garage and enhanced the den space. Again, renovation time would be within sixty to ninety days and cost will depend on the overall size of the project."

Edi waved her hand and said, "Before we go any further, let's pour our afternoon refreshments and get some of our questions about what you have just showed out in the open."

"Good idea, Edi. This is a good place to pause. If you ladies would like to have your martinis, I will be happy to join you and answer your initial questions. Please remember, the stages we are looking at can be phased in over any time period we agree to, and I would be able to lower your costs considerably once we have determined what you want to do." Stan said this looking at Elli and noting how warm and inviting her eyes were.

At that, Edi got up and went in to the kitchen for the drinks trolley. Elli said to Stan, "I love your sketches. This house would look like a showplace with just these changes."

Stan wanted very much to ask her out to dinner, but how to do it without offending Edi?

Edi was back with the trolley. As they drank, Stan continued, showing his third sketch of the second floor addition and then finally, the fourth sketch of the completed Cape Cod with the while window frames and red front door. "As I said at the beginning, time isn't an issue. We can plot each project stage when it fits your schedule and your financial situation. I am not as interested in time as I am in designing a warm, distinctive home that will stand out in the neighborhood and make its own unique statement."

Edi was the first to speak. "Elli, please replenish our glasses before we begin our discussion. We certainly have a lot to cover. Stan, you have given us exciting food for thought."

"That is an encouraging comment, Edi. What do you both think of my designs for your home? Are they in line with your own thoughts?"

Sipping slowly, Edi began the conversation. "Stan, I am overwhelmed by your sketches. Our humble cottage becomes like something out of *Architectural Digest*. How can we possibly afford this?"

"Let me assure you, we can keep costs down and spread payments over any length of time that will work for you. I have to tell you ladies, I am enthusiastic about this project. As most of the renovations have been completed on Maple Drive, your home would be my signature landmark showplace." As he said this, he put down his empty glass; and looking into Elli's eyes, he said, "Let me take both of you to dinner tonight so we can continue our discussion. Are you available?"

Edi was an astute woman. She had watched the growing attraction between Stan Baxter and Elli. She cared very deeply for Elli and wanted only happiness for her friend, especially as she had had such an unhappy marriage. She also knew that there was nothing more uncomfortable than being the third wheel at dinner. No, she would excuse herself and let Elli and Stan go to dinner and continue discussing their home improvements. She trusted Elli not to give away their social hour fun.

"Oh, Stan, how very nice of you. Unfortunately, I have other plans for this evening, but I think Elli can go, can't you, dear?"

"Well, Edi, if you have other plans, then I would be happy to have dinner with you, Stan. Bring the sketches so we can review them. I have many questions."

"Stan, why don't you come by about seven o'clock and pick up Elli? By then we will have gone over them, and she can share both of our thoughts and questions with you."

After Stan had left, promising to be back at seven o'clock, Edi said to her friend. "Elli, things have gotten a bit complicated. What started out as a little fun sharing our martini hour with sample salespeople and building contractors has moved into much more. Elli, are you personally interested in Stan Baxter? Because it seems to me that you might be, and if you are, we should stop inviting other contractors in.

"I know you had a difficult marriage and certainly deserve to enjoy a compatible relationship with someone who can take good care of you. Stan might be that someone. I just want you to do what will make you happy. After all, we are sisters, aren't we?"

As Edi spoke, Elli stared at the slight misty rain coating the living room window. She turned to look at her friend. There were tears in her eyes, and her voice was soft as, with a shy smile, she said to her friend, "Oh, Edi, what a wonderful sister you are. I will admit I find Stan a warm, kind, and endearing man. It is hard to think of him as one of our social hour guests."

"Go with your heart. Have dinner with him and spend time with him if that is what you both want. Let the relationship build naturally. If it develops into something, well then, it means it is meant to be. I want only the best for you, dear friend."

Chapter 4

As Edi and Elli were having this heartfelt talk, Stan was anxiously planning what he would say to Elli. He really wanted this to blossom into a lasting relationship. He didn't want to lose this chance at happiness. Now as he was in his midsixties, he thought how wonderful it would be to have the lovely Elli at his side. He envisioned taking trips and enjoying warm, cozy evenings together. He would take his time to build this relationship carefully. He didn't want to lose this special lady.

* * *

Elli and Stan were sitting at a cozy table illuminated by candles and warmed by the coals of a nearby fireplace. "Elli, before we begin to go through these sketches, I would like to get to know a bit more about how the two of you ended up sharing the cottage—if this isn't too personal, that is."

Elli paused and then she smiled and swirled her wineglass as she said, "Edi and I were best friends all through college. We had a special bond and even though our marriages took us to far different parts of the country, we kept in touch. When my husband died, I wrote Edi and came for a visit that ended in our agreeing to live together. So we became sisters again. It is a wonderful friendship, and we enjoy being together."

"So you are old friends enjoying a renewed friendship," Stan said. "Well I hope my sketches can create the kind of place that will give you room to share as well as space for your own personal privacy when you want it."

"That fits our needs so well. After all, being in our midsixties doesn't mean our life is over. We enjoy going out to dinner, the movies, concerts, and lots of events in the park at the end of Maple Drive."

Stan had learned what he needed to know. Elli was close to his age and liked the same kind of activities he did. He smiled at Elli, and as he refilled her wineglass, he said, "I hope this is the beginning of more activities for us—and of course, for Edi too."

They spent the rest of the dinner reviewing the sketches, with Stan reassuring Elli that the project could be spread out over time to suit their needs. The only hesitation he noted was when he started to talk about when they would like to start. "This is something Edi and I will have to discuss. I hope you can be a little patient with us, Stan."

"Of course, you need to decide this together. I just want you to know that I am eager to help, and I will tell you why. You see, I am thinking of slowing down, letting some of my team take over the day-to-day operations and client meetings. I want this to be my final signature project. I want to start taking time for travel and relaxing in a home I can build with someone with whom I can share it."

As he said this, he paused to see what effect his words had on Elli, hoping she had read his underlying message. He continued. "My wife passed away a number of years ago, and my two sons are eager to take over the business. And frankly I am ready to let them. My only concern is living without having someone to share my life with. I must admit I am a bit envious of the warm relationship you and Edi have."

"I am the truly lucky one, Stan. Edi took me in when I found myself in a financial bind when my husband died. She helped me get back on my feet, and for this I will be forever thankful."

"Perhaps we can be more than just business partners, Elli. We can be good friends and perhaps share some pleasant plays and concerts together. Of course, we would include Edi, if you wish."

Elli smiled up at Stan and said, "I am having such a good time. I know Edi just wants me to be happy, and right now, I truly am."

* * *

Edi watched Stan walk Elli to their door. He kissed her cheek and turned down the walkway. Elli came in. Her eyes were sparkling, and there was a smile on her lips. Edi decided to let her friend tell her about the evening. Elli began by talking about the lovely dinner they had had and how Stan was looking forward to retiring, letting his sons take over the day to day operations. She added that he wanted their house to be his signature project. She finally paused, and Edi commented, "Sounds as if you had a grand dinner. Did he try to get you to agree to his renovating our house?"

"I think he was inferring that when he mentioned that he wanted this to be his final project and that his sons would be taking over his business. Oh, and I didn't give away our little social hours or our visits with other contractors. I was very careful to let him know that you and I made all our decisions together. The only personal thing that came up was when he said he would like to take us to a play or a concert."

"I am sure he added me as an afterthought," Edi remarked dryly. "I think we had better take some time before we do anymore with Mr. Baxter. Right now we have to plan for the Tennetti Brothers. They are coming in a few days, and we need to plan that meeting."

They spent the rest of the evening discussing the upcoming Tennetti meeting. Before retiring for bed, both had agreed that they would ask for an estimate on changing the two front windows into little bay windows and putting a porch over the front door. Since the Tennetti firm hadn't done any work on Maple Drive, both girls were sure they would be eager to get a job that would put them on the now-prestigious street.

The following Tuesday, a somewhat-dusty brown pickup truck came to a stop in the drive way of number 610. The driver—a short, red-faced man with a squat pair of legs—came around the front of the truck as his brother—another heavyset man with skin burned by too many years in the sun—slid off the other side of the truck's front seats and looked over the front of the house.

"Joe, what do these ladies want us to do? Just remind me, 'cause this doesn't look like much of a house to me."

Joe, the shorter of the two brothers, replied, "They said something about putting in bay windows and a front porch. And if that is what they want, we will have to tell them that it will mean we'd have to repaint the whole house."

At that moment, Elli opened the front door and said, "Hello, you must be the Tennetti Brothers. Please come in, won't you?"

"Sure, lady. You got a nice place here. Pete and I just need to get a better idea of what you want and why you called us when there are lots of other contractors already working on this street."

His frankness took Elli a bit by surprise, and she quickly changed her judgment of the shrewdness of the brothers. "You know, you are quite right to ask this question. Let me introduce the other homeowner to you, and we can get down to business."

At this moment, Edi, having heard the question, replied, "One quick answer to your question is just what you have already brought up. There are a lot of builders and contractors already working and charging more than we can afford to make the kind of changes we want. We are hoping your pricing will be more reasonable since you aren't working on our street at this time. You see we have two windows that look out from our den and our living room. We want to turn each into bay windows and put a little porch over the front door. It would dress our house up a bit, don't you think?"

Pete was walking around the two front windows and the area where the front door stood. He took out a steel measuring tape and measured the width of the windows and the space of the front door. "You know, we would have to take out part of this flooring and even out the level of the rest of the floors. In addition to adding the bay windows and a little porch, we would have to repaint the shingles so the house looks the same front to back."

"Oh my, we need to talk about all you think we need to do. Just so you know, we are widows on a strict budget. That is why we picked you. We thought you might be less costly than the other contractors." Then, looking at Elli, she added, "We usually have a little refreshment about now. Would you care to join us?"

Both men grinned and nodded.

"Elli, would you bring our martini trolley out? We usually like a martini about now. Would you gentlemen join us?" When Edi saw the men look a bit confused by her invitation, she quickly changed tack. "If martinis aren't your drink of choice, what can we get for you?"

Joe looked at Pete and said, "If you gals want to have a little afternoon drink, we would be glad to join in with what we like. Pete, go out to the truck and get a six-pack or two of Bud. That ought to do us."

And so a delightful afternoon was spent with the four of them sketching out what the Tennetti Brothers could do for minimal cost. Elli kept reminding everyone that the brothers' sign would go up in the front yard so everyone could see who was doing the renovation. Other business was sure to follow. A tentative agreement was reached pending the cost estimate that was to follow.

Chapter 5

After the Tennettis' truck cleared the driveway, Edi turned to Elli and said that they were really knowledgeable builders, and if their costs were doable, they should consider making this renovation. Elli looked skeptically at her friend and commented that if they really did this, they would have to end any further contractor visits with martini social hours.

"Oh, of course you are right. I just got carried away. I forgot the real purpose of our contacts with the contractors and builders. Anyway, that was a fun social hour, wasn't it? By the time we got all the work done that they said we needed to do, we might as well tear our little cottage down and start over! I think we need to take a break and wait until we hear from them and also see what your next step will be with Stan Baxter."

* * *

Although the crowd at Archie's Bar and Grill was pretty loud, Joe and Pete managed to talk huddled over their beers. Joe said, "When you consider we would have to do two coats of paint over their whole house 'cause it is so old and you add on the leveling of the flooring, I think twenty-five thousand is a fair price to quote them. What do you think, Pete?"

"We can make it more acceptable to them if we let them make payments over a series of months. That might be too much for them to pay all at once. Call them tomorrow. Give them our estimate, and tell them we are willing to space out payments over time."

* * *

Elli was out mowing their lawn when Joe Tennetti called. "Hello, Mrs. Harris, Joe Tennetti here. Say, have you got an e-mail address? I could e-mail our estimate to you, and then we could discuss it over the phone. Save you and us time."

Edi replied, "Mr. Tennetti, we don't have a computer or e-mail or whatever you are asking about. You can mail it to us or bring it over for our review. I am sorry, but we are not up on all this technology."

"Tell you what, we'll stop by on our way home from our current job. Would five o'clock be OK with you?"

"That will be fine. Elli and I will be eager to see what you have come up with. See you about five o'clock."

Edi went out and shared with Elli the conversation she had just had with Joe Tennetti. Both girls were interested. They had previously agreed that they would thank the brothers and tell them they would have to think about it. They would eventually respectfully decline.

It was just after five o'clock that afternoon that Joe and Pete pulled up in their old brown pickup truck. Elli opened the door and waved them in. Joe handed over a copy of the cost estimate. They explained that the total covered the two coats of paint over the whole house as well as the leveling and additions to the flooring and the new bay windows and roof over the little front porch. When Joe had finished the review of the estimate, he asked if they wanted a beer while they discussed the bid.

"Oh, I think not, as it is too close to dinner," replied Edi. She shook her head and said that twenty-five thousand dollars was more than they could afford. Pete jumped in, saying," We would be willing to let you make a series of payments over time so the cost wouldn't strain your budget. How would that be?"

Elli looked at Edi and said in almost a resigned voice, "You know, we always discuss any financial situation to make sure we are in agreement. This is less, I am sure, than the other contractors and builders would charge, but we still need to talk this over and get back to you. Would that be all right with you?"

"Look, ladies, we have given you a fair price and told you we are willing to spread your payments out over time. What more do you want?"

"I am sure you are being fair with us. It is just that twenty-five thousand is a lot of money for us to commit to. Give us a few days, and we will get back to you with our final decision. Would that be acceptable to you?"

"Well, I guess that will have to do. I speak for both Pete and me that I had hoped we could sign this up and start planning the project. Just don't wait too long, as we have some other projects in the works," Joe said as he gathered their papers together prior to leaving.

Over dinner that evening, Edi remarked that she felt a little anxious about telling Joe and Pete that they weren't going ahead with the project at the present time. She knew the brothers would think they were getting the runaround, and in a way, they were. What was a game for the two girls was how these men made their living, not something to take lightly. "The least we can do is promise them that if we decide to make this renovation in the future, it will definitely be with them."

The next morning Stan Baxter called. He wanted to set up a brief meeting before he took Elli out for dinner that evening. "I found a problem we will have to resolve before we do any renovation. You know in my sketches how I have expanded the house using the garage as part of the den? Well that won't work given the size of your lot. I will show you when I get there. Would three o'clcok be all right? Good, see you then."

At three o'clock the three of them looked at the sketch of the house with the expansion of the den into the current garage. "Here's the problem, Stan said, your lot is 40 feet wide by 130 feet deep. These renovations just will not fit on this lot. We either have to scale everything back or build you a new house on another piece of property, like the vacant property at the end of Maple Drive."

After Stan had left for his office, Edi turned to Elli and said, "Oh dear, what have we gotten ourselves into? What started as fun martini social hours now seems out of our control. It was all right to put off salespeople who were just showing us samples of their products. After all, their loss was a bit of time and a possible future sales opportunity. And I think most of them enjoyed the little martini hour they spent with us. But when we started meeting with the contractors, it was like we were leading them on. They were spending more than just time, they were developing real plans and projecting costs that would affect their personal income. We are in over our heads. Oh my goodness, I just had a thought! Could what we are doing be considered illegal?"

"Calm down, Edi. You are overreacting. Since no money has changed hands, all we are guilty of is wasting their time in addition to providing them with free martinis. I think we need to stop our calls and meetings with the contractors. If anyone calls, we will simply tell them personal 'family' business has come up and we need to deal with that for now. We will have to continue with Stan because he has invested more than just time. And besides, I do like him and enjoy having dinner with him. For now, all calls and visits with other builders and contractors are off-limits. Do you agree?"

"Absolutely. Since I started the contact with the Tennetti Brothers, I will be the one to call them. I will use your idea of having some personal family issues that have arisen, and when we can, we will definitely get back in touch. I am sure they have had other people delay going forward. After all, not everyone begins a project even when the offer is valid and good. I do agree that we should stop and start having our own quiet martini hours by ourselves for a while. In fact, it is about time for us to enjoy an afternoon martini right now."

"Elli, you are right. Now we are being sensible. We have a lot to talk about. Will you do the honors? I am going to get a notebook so we can strategize next steps. I also think you should tell me what the situation is between you and Stan. How serious are you about him?"

As twilight settled over the maple trees and the sky turned a pale mauve, Elli looked at Edi and said, "I really like him. He is quiet, attentive, and caring. When we walk into a restaurant, you can see people glancing at us. He walks like the athlete he once was and is still slim and trim. Even with the gray flecks in his brown hair, he appears young and vital. I will admit I think I would marry him, if he would ask me. Does that upset you, Edi?"

"No, of course not. Like I have said many times, we are sisters, and I want what is best for you. If your relationship turns into marriage, I intend to be your maid of honor and help give you away!

"In the meantime. Let's enjoy this lovely evening. Oh, by the way, did I tell you that I am going to meet Opal Webster and Sandra Richter at the library tomorrow? They want to discuss an idea for a new heritage museum. You remember meeting them at the last council meeting. They are the grand dames of Maple Drive—in on everything and wanting to make Maple Drive the social center of Bexley."

"Just don't volunteer us for any of their charity drives or events. The last time, I loaded over one hundred cans of pickled peaches into cartons for one of their little community auctions. Oh, and don't get yourself involved in one of their little charity drives where you have to go house to house seeking donations to turn Maple Drive into a gated community. The last time they tried to do this, they divided all the neighbors into two groups—one wanting to make themselves feel special and the other, including us, not wanting to be so snobbish," remarked Elli.

Edi laughed and told her not to worry. This meeting had to do with creating a Bexley heritage museum. This certainly seemed like a worthy endeavor. "After all, this was a worthwhile project, and we both can see the value in it. Why, this may make our little old cottage part of the museum."

* * *

While this conversation was going on, Opal and Sandra were having their own conclave in Seaver's Coffee Shoppe. Opal and Sandra lived next door to each other. Opal and her husband, Ralph, had built a French-like chateau, and Sandra and her husband, Sam, had erected a mock Tudor minimansion complete with a garden maze and fountain. Both women became fast friends, wanting Bexley to consider Maple Drive as the center of Bexley's social life. Their husbands worked for investment firms in Bloomington. They wanted their wives to host parties and balls to gain new customers and cement their place as important members of the community. It was Opal who first saw the possibilities of Edi's shabby little cottage. She had remarked to Sandra that it just might have some historical significance. Sandra had been researching Bexley's history and found out that the Edith Harris cottage was the first house built on what was once Maple Street. That was in 1939, at the beginning of World War ll. During the war years and immediately after in the 1950s, the street filled up with bungalows and small-framed ranch houses. Bexley still was a small town then. It wasn't until the 1970s, when the economy was booming, that Maple Street was turned into Maple Drive and the gentrification of the homes began. Commuters for the businesses in both Terre Haute and Bloomington started moving into Bexley, which was midway between the two cities.

"You know, Opal," said Sandra Richter, "the Harris cottage could be turned into a little heritage museum that tells the story of the part our town played during the war and after. Why, people living here worked in the plants making bombers and jeeps for the war effort. We were vital as a shipping center for rubber being sent to the tire factories in Cleveland, Ohio, and for auto parts needed in Detroit. Back then, Bexley buzzed with activity, and it can again, if we develop a heritage museum and host historical tours. We can have advertising about our town as a worthwhile tourist stop in our part of Indiana."

"I can see billboards featuring Bexley as part of America's contribution to winning the Second World War. How exciting is that! We will be creating new business for our town and making it an important place to stop and visit. Why, this might even cause the town council to consider having a hotel built. But before we get any further down this path, we have to get Edith Harris to agree to turn her home into the heritage museum. We can get some sort of apartment built in the back of the museum lot for her. After all, I think we should appoint her heritage administrator or curator or whatever they call someone who manages a museum. We need to talk with Ralph and Sam and see if they think we should pay her a small salary for doing this. Don't you think so, Sandra?"

"Yes, I do, Opal. I am just glad my interest in history has been so beneficial. All my research has paid off. I will continue to go back through old records and make sure we have all we need to make our town a valuable part of Indiana's history. When are we meeting with Edith?"

"The meeting is tomorrow in the town library. I thought that was a good place to meet as we are going to be talking about making new history for our town!"

Their sleek frosted hairdos bobbed up and down as they talked and sipped their coffee. Both Opal and Sandra tried their very best to look smart and sophisticated. Why, when hot pants and go-go boots were the fashion, they were the first to appear in them. Right now they were clothed in pastel pantsuits and over-the-shoulder flowered scarfs. After all, they were the leading socialites in Bexley. As the afternoon wore on, they began to plan a special session of the town council, which they both ran, to discuss the funding of this new project. They were sure they could get the other council members to see the future value of this project to their town.

"The funding might be in the form of a levy or addition to the property taxes or whatever," said Sandra airily. "Once we show the council the benefits that will come from this effort, they will be sure to go along with it," she added. "We mustn't forget about Edith Harris. We will have to get her on board and willing to sell her house."

Opal nodded and added, "We should ask our husbands what they think the house is worth. And we should not forget that if we make her the administrator or curator or whatever, she will be getting a salary, so we had better ask them what she should get. Oh dear, we have a lot to do to get this project off the boards!"

* * *

The library had been built in the 1950s. It was an impressive building of granite with Ionic columns along the front. Going up the steps to the front doors made one feel as if they were entering an important government building. But once you entered, the row upon row of dusty books and the dry papery smell made you forget its imposing facade. In addition to the main room, there were side rooms with desks and tables for readers to use. It was in one of those rooms that Opal and Sandra met with Edi. Edi knew the two women from all their community involvement, but this was the first time she had met with them personally.

Opal began their discussion by saying she had heard Edith had a friend living with her. "Is this just a social visit, or is she a permanent guest to your lovely old cottage, Edith?"

Edith expressed surprise. She said, "I am not sure what that has to do with me talking to you about building some sort of Bexley museum."

"But that is exactly what we do want to talk about, Edith. We, along with the town council, intend to create a Bexley Heritage Museum where we can display artifacts, photographs, and signs showing our contribution to the growth of our country over the years, especially the years prior to and through the Second World War. Sandra has unearthed a lot of material that shows how vital we were, and we think your cottage—which best represents Bexley during that time—would be the ideal place to locate the Bexley Heritage Museum. Don't you see how it just fits ideally into the Bexley story?" Opal said as she smiled brightly at Edi.

"Before I answer you, just what has that got to do with my house guest? She happens to be an old college friend who has moved in with me to share my home. We are like sisters."

"Oh dear, that poses a problem. I don't suppose she will be moving out then," remarked Opal.

"I don't think that is any of your business," Edi said hotly.

Before she could say any more, Sandra broke in. "Edith please don't get upset. We seem to have handled this poorly. Let me explain what we are interested in doing, and you will see why we asked you these questions."

Edi calmed down and said, "All right, let's start over. What did you want to see me about?"

Sandra continued. "Thank you, Edith. You see, we have been researching the history of Bexley and amassed a lot of material that tells the story of our town especially its involvement in supporting our country during the war. We got together with the town council and bounced the idea of creating a Bexley Heritage Museum. They were not only in agreement but quite excited about the idea, as it would help make our town a tourist destination. We want to display all the artifacts, especially the photographs and records we have uncovered. There is quite a lot of material. We thought the right place to display all of this would be in your lovely old cottage, which is the last of the homes built prior to the war. Of course, we would want you to be the administrator or curator of the museum. We would provide a salary and have even talked about putting in a small apartment in the backyard for you."

"So you can see why we asked you about your house guest," Opal said, picking up the conversation from Sandra. "As we see it, there just wouldn't be room for both of you in the small apartment we have in mind. Of course you would be busy running the museum, leaving little time for your friend."

"Does this make things clearer for you?" Opal asked this and then stopped to give Edi a chance to reply.

"Yes, it does. You want me to be the curator of Bexley's proposed heritage museum, living in the backyard in an efficiency apartment. For this I will receive a salary, to be determined by the council. My main occupation will be to act as a guide inside the museum for tourists stopping in Bexley on their way either to Terre Haute or Bloomington. Have I got this right?

"How much will I be paid for my home? Whom will I be accountable to, and how will the museum be cared for? Will there be a maintenance staff to take care of everything?"

Sandra pursed her lips and said in a slightly annoyed tone, "Well, at the beginning of any project like this, there are bound to be lots of loose ends to attend to, so we haven't the answers to all these questions you are posing. We just wanted you to know that the council thinks you are the ideal person to head this up and help develop it."

Chapter 6

Edi left the two women, saying she would think about their offer and would be interested in the answers they had for the questions she had asked. She was angry and felt their high-handed way of treating her personal life and that of her friend was insulting. They seemed to think they were doing her a favor! They definitely didn't know Edith Harris. She had learned a lot from her husband, and she was about to put all of it to work. "Just wait until I tell Elli what this sham meeting was about," she said to herself.

Elli listened to Edi's explanation of what had taken place at the library meeting. When Edi had finished, she commented, "You are right. They were very high-handed in their approach. It would seem that they want you to be a caretaker, living in a small efficiency behind your former home, for which they will pay you a small salary. In the first place, they will have taken over your home, pushed me into limbo, and created a museum no one is going to visit because all they have to show are some old photographs and records from the town council files of what the town did during the war. Who in heaven is going to want to visit it?"

Elli continued, "You know what I think we ought to do? I think we ought to ask Stan what he thinks about this. He has put a lot of time and effort into making Maple Drive the showplace that it is. He will definitely be able to help us. We are going to see him tomorrow to discuss the problem of our lot being too small for the renovations he has suggested. With this idea by the council, all his project plans are worthless. Let's bring him up-to-date on what the council wants to do and see what he thinks we should do. I can tell you one thing he won't like, and that is me being put out on the street!"

* * *

"Stan, I learned from my husband, Henry," Edi said when he arrived to take Elli out, "that you have to be very specific when planning a project with another team or group." Stan had listened as the girls told him about Edi's meeting with Opal and Sandra and their plans for the cottage. He was angry that the council was moving without getting input from the community for one thing. He was also angry because they hadn't thought through the potential of what a Bexley museum could be. Obviously, they needed to put together a team representing the whole community to determine what kind of a museum they might develop.

He said, "Ladies, let us take the lead away from Opal and Sandra. I suggest, Edi, that you go back to them to let them know that as administrator, you have decided to get the whole community involved. You are sending out letters to everyone to get their ideas for what kind of a museum they want in Bexley. You should give them some choices that we can live with. For instance, the Bexley War Years Museum or the American World War II Home Front Museum. In other words, you need to seize control. Tell them you are enthusiastic about what this might mean to Bexley. Mention how you can see additions to local businesses with needs for some restaurants and maybe down the road, even a small heritage hotel. Give them lots of ideas and concepts to get rolled up in. In the meantime, we can go ahead with our plans just as soon as we can get them finalized. Right now, I am taking you to dinner, Elli. While we are gone, start making specific lists of what we need to do, Edi."

"What you are suggesting makes me feel much better. I was just so angry I wasn't thinking rationally. Stan, thank goodness you have become our friend. I am going to make some lists of what needs to be done and some specific questions the council needs to answer."

And with that, Edi sat down at her kitchen table and got to work on her lists. She remembered how Henry had said that in order for a project to be successful, you needed to address what needs to be done, who needs to do it, why it needs to be done, and how it is going to be accomplished. All of this should be as specific as possible so no one can misunderstand the overall mission. With this ringing in her head, Edi got started in earnest, ignoring both Elli and Stan as they left the cottage.

For a change of pace, Stan had taken Elli to a small inn outside of Bexley. It was an Old Coach Inn with a good wine cellar. It had a huge fireplace opening where they used to roast whole pigs and lambs. The fireplace only boasted a delightful fire these days, which gave the dining area a warm, intimate feeling. Their table was beside the fireplace, in a corner under a window that overlooked the gardens outside.

Once the waiter had taken their order and poured the wine, Stan reached over and took Elli's hand. Softly caressing it, he looked into her eyes. "You have become very important to me, Elli. When I wake up in the morning, I think of you and look forward to seeing and being with you. It has been a long time since I have felt this way. I hope you know that I have fallen in love with you."

Stan paused long enough for Elli to respond. "Oh, Stan, I feel the same way about you. I am so happy when I am with you. I have never felt this way before. All my life I have had to be the one keeping things together, never feeling safe, secure, or even appreciated. This feeling I have for you is new to me. If nothing ever happens, your presence in my life will have been enough." As she said this, she put her other hand over his.

Stan's voice was a little rough as he reached up and, caressing her face, said, "Elli, will you complete my life by becoming my wife?"

With tears glistening in her eyes, she said, "Yes, oh yes, Stan."

They both reached over the small table and kissed—a gentle, long kiss.

Both were quiet for a few minutes, then Stan smiled and said, "Well, I think this calls for champagne." He gestured for the waiter and ordered a bottle of Dom Perignon. Once the champagne had been served, he said to Elli, "The only questions I have are when can we be married, and where do you want to live?"

Elli put her champagne glass down. She was smiling as she said, "If it were possible, I would marry you as soon as we could and live in the house you have now." Before Stan could say anything, she added, "Edi has told me that if you and I should marry, she would be my maid of honor and give me away. There is one thing you should know—I do want to help her to save her home or start a drive to make it a worthwhile museum. She helped me in my hour of need, and I want to help her now."

Stan nodded in understanding and said, "Of course we will help her. I think the suggestions I have already given should get us off to a good start. You may have noticed, I included myself in on the museum project. After all, we are a team now."

As they sipped their champagne, Elli said, "Stan, you know all about me, I have told you my life story during the dinners we have had. Now, I want to know more about you. Things like where you were born, where you went to school, if you had brothers and sisters, how you ended up in the construction business . . . even about your first marriage. I want to know all about the man I am going to marry."

Stan leaned back in his chair. He smiled at Elli and said, "So you want to know all about me, do you? Are you afraid there are skeletons in my closet? Well, don't worry. Up until now, my life is pretty much like most guys'. My parents were from Terre Haute. They raised three boys. I was the youngest. My brother Cal was killed in Korea, and my brother Ed still lives in Terre Haute. He's a CPA there. I went to the local schools and did well enough in football to get a scholarship to Notre Dame. I played football there. My only claim to fame was catching a pass and running forty yards to make the winning touchdown in a championship game. I studied architecture and when I graduated. I went to work for a local architect here in Bexley. We designed homes and office buildings. After a few years, I made the transition to doing the actual building and started my own construction company. Along the way, I married my high school sweetheart, Sharon, and we raised two sons. Both boys are married and have their own families. They work with me and are champing at the bit to take over the business. Sharon developed leukemia and passed away four years ago. End of story."

Chapter 7

"I am so sorry you lost your first wife. I am sure you were a good husband and father, and I promise I will do my best to make you happy for rest of our lives together." After Ellie finished, she took a sip of her champagne and looked expectantly at Stan.

"I have wanted to be with you since I first met you. You and I will have a wonderful life together. I want to build us the Cape Cod house I designed. I have already purchased the vacant land at the end of Maple Drive overlooking the pond. There is enough land there for me to add a second small Cape Cod cottage nearer the pond for Edi. How does this sound to you, Elli?"

Elli put both hands over her eyes for a minute before she replied. "It all sounds wonderful. You have made me so happy. May I share all this with Edi when I get home tonight? I know she will be thrilled that I am going to marry you."

For the rest of the evening, the two of them discussed wedding plans, honeymoon locations, possible dates—even who they should invite. At last, long after the inn had emptied, they left with Stan's arm around Elli and her head on his shoulder.

Edi stood at the kitchen window drinking her coffee. It was early morning and she was tired. She had spent the evening developing lists of things that needed to be done in order for Bexley to develop a first-class museum. She had prioritized and reprioritized all of it until she had a working plan. The next step was to go over it with Elli and Stan to make sure she hadn't left anything out.

Just then, she heard Elli come into the kitchen. She turned and smiled and said, "I fell asleep before you came in last night. How was your dinner at the Old Coach Inn?"

Elli could hardly contain herself. "Oh, Edi, it was the most magical night of my life. Stan asked me to marry him, and I said yes! We want to have a small wedding with a reception at the country club where Stan is a member. He is going to build the Cape Cod house he designed for us to live in! It is going to be on the vacant land near the pond in the park at the end of Maple Drive, and he is going to build a Cape Cod cottage for you on the same land, only nearer the pond. I am so excited. I can't believe I am going to have such a wonderful future married to such a wonderful man.

She finally slowed down enough for Edi to interject. "This is absolutely the best news. Remember, I am your maid of honor, and I want to plan the reception. The country club will be the perfect place."

"Stan says it has a lovely events room and an experienced chef who is used to handling wedding receptions. I think that would be a good place, and you can work with the chef to select the food, cake, and decorations. You know, Edi, if it hadn't been for you taking me in and letting me live with you, I would never have met Stan. You have encouraged me and supported me, and I love you so much. You truly are my sister."

With that said, the girls hugged and left to get dressed and ready for the busy day ahead.

Outside, the last of the winter snow fell, only to melt as it hit the ground. It was clear that winter was making its last try, but on the ground, buds were emerging, and the grass was a rich green. The forsythia were blooming, and the sky was bright with sunlight. Spring was arriving just in time to grace the upcoming wedding.

Elli, Stan, and Edi were sitting in the den working on the wedding plans. Elli said, somewhat sadly, "I have no one to put on the list. My parents are gone, and I have no other family. I am all alone." Stan reached over and put a hand on her shoulder. "Honey, you will never be alone again. Edi and I are your family now. We will have a small wedding and reception. After all, I just have my sons and their families and my brother and his wife."

Edi took notes of these names and then looked up to say, "Well, we have a number of people we have to invite from town. For example, we have to invite Opal and Sandra and Mrs. Audrey Preston—she's our leading socialite so we can't ignore her. Oh, also Mary Arnoult who writes the social column in the *Bexley News*. There are a number of people who are helping us with our community drive in support of the museum. But perhaps I am missing the purpose here. This isn't a community activity—it is your wedding, and it should be small and intimate. I will make up a list for you two to look over, and once we have agreed on the invitees, I will make out the invitations. I can start as soon as you have gotten a date set at the church."

"We have asked the minister to let us know if March 16 is available. That gives us a month to plan everything and get the invitations sent out. I am responsible for planning the honeymoon, which I am already working on, so you and Elli need to take over the wedding and reception. Don't worry about costs. I can take care of that," Stan said. "Now if you ladies have nothing else you need from me, I am going to see how my sons are doing with our construction projects—of course, one being our new house. They promised they would have the flooring laid out and will pour the concrete slab in the next day or two. Before I go, I just thought of two people I want you to invite. They are old friends of mine, Buddy Tranchina, whom I play golf with, and Coach Brown who runs the pro shop at the country club. Over the years, he has been responsible for improving my golf game, so I owe him bigtime." With that Stan kissed Elli and left.

Edi and Elli got busy planning the wedding. They called the country club and reserved the room for the reception and set a date to meet with the chef to plan the food and drinks. They also set a date and time to go to the local bridal shop to select a dress for Elli and something for Edi. "Phew, that is enough for today. Besides, it is time for a little liquid refreshment."

"I will do the honors and fix us each a martini to celebrate your upcoming nuptials," Edi said.

As they sat in the living room enjoying their drinks, Elli remarked, "It is so hard to take everything in. In little less than a year, I have gone from having nothing, living with you, and trying to do what I could to pay you back for taking me in to being Stan's fiancé with the prospect of having a lovely wedding and living in a dream home at 1200 Maple

Drive. That's the street address for the new Cape Cod home Stan's building. Isn't life absolutely amazing!"

"You just never know what the future holds," Edi said. "Based on Stan's advice, I have managed to gain the upper hand with Opal and Sandra and the town council. I have already sent out flyers and letters announcing the development of a WWII Home Front museum. I am asking everyone in the community to look through their trunks and attics and see if they can find things to donate that reflect what life was like here at home during the war years. I have received several enthusiastic calls from people wanting to know where to bring their items. Oh, that reminds me—Stan is going to have to get moving on the expansion of my cottage to fit the museum's needs. I am just glad there is an extra bedroom at Stan's place for me."

Stan's sons, Bobby and Rick, had split their teams so that one was working on the expansion of Edith's old cottage to make it the foundation for the new museum. They were expanding the back of it and renovating the rooms to accommodate all the items people were donating that represented Bexley during the war years. In addition, the other main team was pouring the concrete and beginning the building of the Cape Cod for their dad. They had put some other construction on hold so each of these projects could be completed quickly.

Elli was busy with the wedding plans. The minister had said that an afternoon wedding at one o'clock would be fine. So the church was all set. Edi was going to put bouquets of white roses, yellow carnations, and daffodils, if she could find them, on each pew and behind the altar.

Both girls had selected wedding outfits. Elli thought it would be more appropriate if she wore a white silk suit with a modest opening at the neck. It flattered her slim figure. She planned to fashion a few flowers in her auburn hair. Something simple but elegant was what she wanted. Edi had selected a pale lilac dress with long sleeves and a heart-shaped neckline. Both girls were completing the wedding list and writing the invitations. Originally, Edi was going to handle the whole wedding herself, but Elli wanted to be involved so the two were working on the invitations.

The list was just complete when the phone rang. It was Sandra Richter. "Hello, Edi? Oh good, Opal and I just want to thank you for the flyers and letters you sent out to everyone. Opal and I are being deluged with phone calls thanking us for suggesting the whole community be involved in our new museum. We want you to go ahead with what you are doing, and we want you to come to the town council meeting tomorrow evening and tell the council what you are planning for the museum and what they can do to get on board with your efforts."

Edi smiled and said, "I would be happy to come and share the plans with the council. After all, they represent our community and need to know what is happening in our town."

After she hung up, she told Elli what Sandra had said. They both laughed and remembered Stan's advice. He was right on the money as usual. Edi decided to let Elli finish the invitations so she could put together notes for her meeting with the council. She wanted to get Stan's advice that evening on how to handle this group.

That evening when Stan arrived, Edi told him about her upcoming meeting with the council. He advised her to take the initiative, deferring to Opal and Sandra by giving them credit for coming up with the museum idea. Once they were mollified by this praise, he told her to go ahead and present their concept for the war years' home front museum filled with all the donations that were beginning to come in from the community. She should get them excited by the idea of Bexley becoming a name on the Indiana map. Tourists from all over will want to come and remember what life was like back then. She should tell them that Stan had provided a storage area where donations would be housed until the museum was complete.

To get the council members further enthused, she should tell them about some of the items that had already been donated. She could even take the toy cars, jeeps, and tanks that the Miller family had provided. She could tell them about the items that had been given by Sam Polaski: blackout drapes and a sand pail used to put out fires. Finally she should tell them about Art Farber's donation. This would make a fitting final story for the council members. Art's father had been drafted in 1943. Both Art and his sister were only five and six years old. Their mother couldn't drive, so their father decided to put his 1940 Ford up on blocks so it would still be good when he came home. He put it in the back of their barn, out of the way. Sadly, he never came home. He died somewhere in France in 1944. The car stayed in the barn all these years. Now Art Farber wanted to donate it to the war years' museum. Stan said, "End with this by saying how it will make a very moving exhibit. Edi, you should ask the council members to search their homes to see if they have anything they might like to donate. Tell them they can call you or Elli with their donations, and someone will pick them up to be stored until we are ready to put them into the museum."

Edi nodded in agreement. "I will do just that. Also, I think it would be a good idea if I revisited those nice sample salespeople who came to see me. Now we can afford to pay them for their products. For example, we are going to need industrial carpets for the museum, and John with Classic Carpets would certainly be a good source for that."

That evening Stan debated whether he should tell Elli about the plans he was making for the honeymoon. He decided he should—if she didn't like what he was planning, it would spoil that special time. "Elli, sit here next to me. I want to tell you what I have in mind for our honeymoon. If you don't like the idea, we can do whatever you want."

Elli nestled against his shoulder and said, "I will be happy wherever we go. Just being with you is all that matters."

"That is very nice, dear, but I want this to be something really special. Here's what I have in mind. After the reception, we will drive to the Old Coach Inn and stay the night at their bed and breakfast. We will get up early in the morning and drive to Indianapolis and catch a plane for Sea Island, Georgia, where we will stay at the Cloisters. It is a fine, old elegant inn surrounded by ocean. Since we are making this a short trip, because we are building the house, I will make it up to you once we are settled with a trip to Saint Bart's or another island in the Caribbean. How does that sound?"

Elli reached up and kissed Stan on the cheek. "It sounds absolutely heavenly. I love the idea of staying our first night at the Old Coach Inn where you proposed to me. It makes our first night so much more romantic."

* * *

The council meeting was crowded, and there was a hubbub of the noise people make when they were talking all at the same time. Edi made her way to the podium in front of the council room. She greeted several people just as Opal and Sandra came up. "Edi, we have a standing room only crowd here. So many people are interested in what you are doing with the new museum."

Edi smiled at both ladies. "I am hopeful everyone will be pleased with what I have planned. Shall I start?"

Opal smiled and said, "I will call the meeting to order, and Sandra will introduce you to everyone. She will also remind everyone of the purpose of this meeting."

A gavel sounded, and Opal called the meeting to order. She then deferred to Sandra, who said, "Thank all of you for coming to this special council meeting. I think the large attendance we have tonight shows how interested the town is in our new museum. Let me turn the meeting over to Edith Harris, who is our new administrator and curator for the museum. Edith?"

Edi graciously thanked Opal and Sandra, reminding everyone that it was because of Opal's and Sandra's original ideas that the whole museum project had started. She paused and started clapping, and the whole audience joined in. Opal and Sandra beamed and nodded their thanks.

"From the beginning, it became evident to me that this museum, which is to be a tribute to what happened on the home front during World War II, needed to represent our whole community. That is why I sent out the flyers and letters telling you about our future WWII Homefront Museum. As you know, I asked each of you to look in your attics, basements, and trunks for items that could be donated for display in the museum. To date, I have received a number of such items, some of which I have brought to show you tonight."

Edi lifted a small box up and took our several little toy cars, tanks, and jeeps. They were scuffed and had some paint missing. "These were toys belonging to Steve Henchel and his brother during the war. Their father served in the Pacific and died there while his sons played with these at home in Bexley."

She paused for a moment to allow everyone to take in her words. Then she went on. "I have received a gold star flag which belongs to the Sam Miller family. They lost their dad in the Battle of the Bulge, and his mother hung the flag proudly in the front window. We will display it with honor. Finally I want to tell you that the Baxter Construction firm is rapidly renovating and expanding my old home as the foundation for the museum. They have also donated a large flagpole to hold the

American Flag and the Indiana Flag which will stand in front of our new WWII Home Front Museum.

"Before I end this, I would like to share with you yet another donation. It is being donated by Art Farber and his family." With this she held up a large photograph of a car on blocks. "Art was six when his dad was called up. Because his sons were just five and six, and his wife couldn't drive, his father decided to put his 1940 Ford up on blocks. He put it in the back of the family barn, planning to bring it out when he came home. Like so many others, he never returned. The car stayed in the back of the barn all these years. Now the Farbers have donated it to the museum, where it will be placed on the ground floor, reminding everyone of what happened during the war years here at home.

"There is one other donation I want to share with you tonight. Some of you might remember the Benson Cinema that closed a number of years ago. Mildred Stephens, whose father owned the movie house, found a trunk of old sixteen millimeter reels of film. She took them to a company in Indianapolis who screened them. They were films of life here in Bexley during the 1940s. She has had them digitalized and given them to our museum. We are going to add a small theater on the second floor and intend to show the eighteen-minute film every half hour. I am sure all of you who lived here during that time will want to see it, to see if your family was caught on this film."

People exchanged nods and looked up as Edi continued. "I hope each of you will look for items that we might place in our new museum. Each item will have a card with the name of the donor on it. Now let me stop to see if there are any questions."

For the next half hour, Edi answered questions from people asking if items they had would be suitable for the museum. She suggested they call her at her office or come and see her. She had set up a temporary office in the Baxter Construction offices where she also had a storage warehouse for all donations. When the meeting finally ended, there was a feeling of enthusiasm and excitement about what they were creating for their town.

Just before Edi left the meeting, Opal and Sandra took her aside and said they had come up with an idea. They were going to hold weekly coffee hours in the community to encourage donations and to get more people involved in the museum. "You know, Edith, we feel it is our responsibility to continue to be involved, as we really started this whole idea. Thank goodness we saw the value it would be for our town, and we were so right in selecting you to be in charge of bringing it to life."

Edi smiled and said, "Thank you for choosing me to handle the organizing and developing of our town's museum. I know we are going to do our town proud with what we are building." On that note, Edi left the council meeting and headed to her temporary home.

Chapter 8

Elli had sent out the wedding invitations. When she was finally done addressing them, she found that they had invited sixty people. With this in mind, Edi had met with the club chef and put together a selection of canapes and cheeses, along with a carving station offering sliced beef and turkey with small rolls for making sandwiches. There would be an area featuring fresh fruit and vegetables with dips. All of this was set around the reception hall so people could wander from the bar to the various food venues. There would be tables and chairs along the sides of the room, and in one corner, Pat Green and her quartet would be playing the soft jazz music that Stan had requested.

As the RSVPs started returning, it became clear that they would have a full crowd at both the church and the reception. The minister had suggested they use the old chapel adjacent to the cathedral, as it could handle the sixty guests very comfortably, whereas the main church would look a trifle vacant with the group of their size. And so they agreed to use the old chapel, which was the first church built in Bexley over a hundred and thirty years ago. It had ornate stained glass windows and plaques along the walls listing the Bexley families who had attended there over the years. Actually, Elli liked it better than the cathedral—it felt more homelike and intimate.

* * *

As February turned into March, hints of spring continued to appear. The grass was a bright green, there were more and more buds on the trees, and here and there, the early flowers were beginning to creep through the old leaves and ground cover. Even the air smelled like spring. The sky no longer looked gray and dull. Puffy clouds raced across the blue sky as the spring wind blew over Bexley. "As my mother used to say to me when I was a little girl, 'God is in his heaven, and all is right with the world,'" said Rachel Binder to her friend as they walked in the park.

Most of the work was done on the interior of the museum. The crew had just completed the upstairs theater and were working on the outside walkways and landscaping. They had even installed the flagpole and flags. The signage was expected within a week. It was just then that a situation loomed.

It was on that Friday that a TV truck pulled up in front of the museum. The truck was followed by a black SUV. The doors of the car opened, and out stepped Tom Carson, Democratic state representative for the local district. He conferred with the TV announcer and then walked over to the front of the museum. The bright lights of the television camera came on, and the announcer said, "We are here in Bexley, in front of a new museum that will soon bring new attention to our beautiful state. Here is State Representative Tom Carson to tell us all about it."

Tom took the microphone and with a broad smile said, "Thank you, Jim. I am really proud to be able to let the public know what we are building in the town of Bexley. Going up behind me is a museum honoring our home front and how it supported our fighting boys during the years of World War II. As you all know, the Democratic Party was the party led by Franklin Delano Roosevelt that won that war for America. I can only say I am proud to be part of that same Democratic Party, and today I am standing in front of one of our tributes to all those who stayed home and fought the war from their front porches. We will be opening this museum soon, and I hope all of Indiana and even the Midwest takes the time to come see what we have built here."

The camera lights went out and Carson reentered his SUV and followed the television truck back toward the state highway.

"The nerve of that guy! Can you believe it? He is taking credit for our museum, saying the Democrats came up with the idea. Call the paper and tell them I want to write an editorial refuting everything he insinuated in his little two-minute speech!" fumed Edi.

Both Stan and Elli were in agreement. Elli added, "How dare he take credit for what our town is building. Make sure you include something about not voting for him in the next election, Edi."

Edi's editorial was read by almost everyone in the community, and it wouldn't be a surprise to anyone if Tom Carson lost the next election. He had tread on the community's pride, and they would not forget it.

* * *

Early March past in a flurry of activity. Stan was pleased with the way the house was coming along. Elli was working with a decorator selecting rugs, tables, chairs, a desk for Stan's home office, a leather couch, and matching club chairs. Whenever she could, she used one of the salespeople who had showed their samples to Edi. Each time, she was gratified that they remembered the "lady who served martinis while she looked at their product." They all were pleased to be able to service Elli.

Suddenly, it was March 15, the day before the wedding. As Elli lay down for the night, she thought of how much her life had changed in the past year. She was thankful to Edi for helping to make tomorrow possible. She smiled as she thought of Stan and how much she loved him. He would not be sorry he had married her, she thought. She vowed to make him happy in every way she could. As her eyes finally closed in sleep, her last thoughts were of walking down the aisle to join Stan. In another bedroom, Edi was still up reviewing one of her endless lists to make sure she had done everything she needed to do for the chapel and the reception room at the country club. As she finally lay down to sleep, she thought first about Elli and how happy she was for her. Then she thought, with a tinge of sadness, how much she still missed Henry. She hoped he would be pleased with all she was doing with the wedding and the museum and all.

March 16 dawned bright and sunny. There was a soft breeze drifting through the trees and early budding plants. The bride and groom were having their morning coffee and getting dressed for their big day. Edi was already at the chapel seeing to the flowers on the pews and the bouquets at the altar. Elli arrived at the beauty shop early to have a manicure and pedicure. She was doing her own hair because Stan liked the way she wore it.

The wedding was set for one o'clock, which meant that people would start arriving at the chapel by twelve thirty or so. Stan's two sons were doing double duty. They were ushering and seating people, and they were acting as their father's best men. Edi met Elli in a side room at the back of the chapel. Edi helped Elli arrange a small band of flowers in her hair. "You look lovely, Elli. You look so young and radiant. Does my flower band look OK?"

Time was slipping away. Both girls turned to face the door as they heard the sound of the organ.

"Oh, it is almost time," said Elli.

"Just remember—we are sisters, and we will always be here for each other," replied Edi.

The Baxter boys were helping seat the guests. There were the Millers, the Farbers, and the Dickersons, among others. At a few minutes before the ceremony was about to begin, Mrs. Audrey Preston swanned into the aisle wearing one of her signature large hats; this one resplendent in peacock feathers. She smiled at everyone as she moved down the aisle to a place near the front. Already sitting in a back pew was Mary Arnoult, taking notes on who was coming in. She would be writing up the wedding in her society column in the *Bexley News*.

Stan and his two sons entered a side door and took their places. Just then the wedding march sounded, and everyone turned to watch Elli and Edi walk slowly down the aisle. Elli's eyes were on Stan, and she smiled only for him.

When the minister asked, "Who giveth this woman?" Edi stepped forward and said "I do." And a few minutes later, the ceremony was over. Just like that, lives are changed.

* * *

Edi was in the first car. She needed to get to the country club to make sure all was ready for the reception. Stan and Elli stayed to accept congratulatory remarks from friends in the congregation. Then they left, relaxing in the back of a large town car.

"Well, my dear, are you happy?" asked Stan.

"I am deliriously happy. I love you so much. You look so handsome in that suit. I want this day to never end."

Stan laughed and kissed her lightly on the lips. "I am sure we will enjoy the wedding reception, but I am looking forward more to later when we can be alone as man and wife."

For Elli the reception was a blur. People moving around carrying drinks from the bar, visiting the roast beef carving station for little sandwiches, filling plates with cheese and crackers, vegetables and dip, and skewers of fresh fruit. Elli was too excited to eat anything. She stood next to Stan and sipped champagne.

"It is going so well. We have just the right amount of food, although I am not so sure about the beer, wine, and liquor," said Edi. She left to check on the liquid refreshments.

In the corner of the room, Pat Green and her trio played the soft jazz that Stan liked. It livened the party, and some of the guests crowded around to listen. It was about five o'clock when Stan and Elli quietly slipped away. They took Stan's car and drove off to begin their honeymoon.

"Well, Mrs. Baxter, how does it feel to be married? Before you answer, I want you to know that you have made me a very happy man. I look forward to our life together."

"Well, Mr. Baxter, being your wife is the best thing that has ever happened to me, and I plan to make our life together the best thing that has ever happened to you."

As they pulled in to the parking lot of the Old Coach Inn, Stan kissed Elli, and with his arm around her, they walked in to start their new life.

Chapter 9

Edi smiled as she read the postcard from Elli. She said the Cloisters was a heavenly place. They were taking long walks along the beach and eating dinner under the stars. Putting aside the card, she opened a letter that had come from State Senator Paul Kimble. *I wonder what he wants,* she thought. *Probably a donation of some sort.* The letter was not a solicitation, instead he said he had viewed the TV coverage of Congressman Carson in which he made it sound as if the Bexley museum was a Democratic effort. Senator Kimble wanted to come and visit the museum and lend his support and the support of the Republican Party. "Oh brother," exclaimed Edi. "Now, we have each political party wanting to take credit for what we have started. Well, for now, I am going to ignore both of them. I find it interesting they want to be involved, but they don't want to do anything to help, like providing funding."

That afternoon, Edi went through the storage building housing all the items the community had donated thus far. Every day more came in. She saw blackout curtains and old pails used to hold sand that people kept near their front doors in case of fires from bombs. She leafed through the dozens of ration books and newspaper pages telling stories about the war and the local bond drives. She paused as she looked at the gold star flags—more than one—donated by families who had lost sons in the war. There was also a chipped and rusted red Radio Flyer wagon sitting on the floor. It contained a ball of string, some tinfoil, and several canned jars of what looked like lard. This had been donated by Adam Cox. He wrote that it was his job to go through his neighborhood every week collecting materials for the war effort. Every Saturday, his mother took what he had collected to the high school gym, where it was added to what other children had gathered. All of this was used to build war materiel.

On the last table in the room was the digitized film they would be showing in the second floor theater. As she turned, she noticed an unopened box that had just been delivered. It was from Marian Peavey. The box contained four dolls. Each one was dressed in a different military uniform. Marian's note said that her mother had made many of these dolls to give to the children whose daddies were overseas fighting. She ended saying she hoped they could be used in the museum. Edi made a note to call Marian to thank her for her donation and assure her that they would indeed be used.

As she was leaving the building, like a clap of thunder, a thought came to her. With all her efforts to get donations from everyone else, she had neglected her own things. She and Henry had lived in their house since 1939. All the boxes and trunks from her attic were currently housed in one of the Baxter Construction warehouses. She would call Rick or Bobby and see if she could go through her old boxes and trunks. *Who knows what I might find*, she thought.

* * *

Bobby Baxter opened the warehouse and told Edi to take her time. She could call him on the warehouse phone when she was ready to leave. Edi looked at her things. They had stored her furniture, pictures, suitcases of clothes, and a number of trunks and boxes from her attic. It was these she wanted to open. She ignored the boxes of dishware and pots and pans. She opened one of the trunks. It contained Henry's Air Force uniform and the medals he won for flying combat missions. Since the museum was not about the war itself, these were not suitable for exhibit.

She opened the second trunk and found it contained a lot of Henry's papers about building Boulder Dam, which became Hoover Dam in 1947 after the war. He had been a fledging contractor then, and beside the dam he had built roads from Texas to California. As she got to the bottom of the trunk, she found a manila packet. Inside was a number of war bonds. *Now these*, she thought, *could go on display*. During the war, everyone bought war bonds to help pay for the war. It was the patriotic thing to do back then.

Edi sat down in one of her chairs. She thought about Henry and how much she missed him. She thought about all those years when he was fighting during the war and how she had prayed every night for his safe return and how joyful she was when he came home. Then she thought about all the years he was gone building bridges, dams, and roads in remote places. She had prayed then too. But he had kept in contact, calling every week and coming home every three months, so it wasn't as bad as the war years. She reached down and pressed her hand against the stiff air force uniform in the trunk. "Henry, I miss you so. It seemed as if there was never enough time for us to be together." Slowly, sadly, Edi made her way to the telephone to call Bobby to pick her up.

* * *

Stan and Elli were back from their honeymoon. Elli was still on cloud nine. "I never knew how wonderful it is to be loved by someone who takes care of you and is interested in making you happy. I appreciate every day and can only say that if it wasn't for you, dear Edi, I would probably be living in some drab-one room apartment and working as a clerk somewhere. I would never have met Stan and been able to be a part of his life."

Edi replied, "If you will come down to earth for a while, I would appreciate your help in reviewing the architectural rendering of the ground floor of the museum. We have to start deciding where we want display cases to go. Oh, and we have to determine where we want them to hang the two plexiglass montages we have had made of the dozens of family photos given by Bexley families who lived here during the war."

Soon the girls were deeply involved in discussing the planning of the exhibits.

* * *

March had given way to April, and all the golfers in Bexley who had patiently waited for spring to arrive were eagerly cleaning their clubs and their golf shoes. No one was as eager as Butty Tranchina. He lived for the game. "Stan, it's Butty. Say, listen, I want to try out my new putter. How about you and me meeting at the club for the first eighteen of the year?"

Stan smiled as he listened to his old friend. "Sure, meet you there at one o'clock," he said.

Stan and Butty went back a long way. Butty ran Butty's Burglar Alarm Systems. Every job Stan had done that had involved putting in a sound alarm system included Butty because he was the best in that business. He also was an avid golfer, and the two of them had spent many afternoons hitting the little white balls around the course. Stan just hoped the ground was hard enough for a good game.

"So, how is married life?" asked Butty."

"Couldn't be better. She's the love of my life," said Stan.

"Well, I just hope you can concentrate on your game, because I intend to whip you, old friend."

Stan laughed and said, "Don't be too sure, as I remember I beat you by eight strokes in our last game." As they started the golf cart, Butty said, "Not going to happen this time!" And with that, they drove to the first tee.

* * *

"What a stroke of luck! Talk about excellent timing! Of course, we will miss them, but this is fortunate for our museum." Edi was on the phone talking with Opal, who had called to tell her that the Johnsons, who lived next to the new museum, were selling their home and moving to Florida to be near their daughter and her family. The committee on the council had agreed to fund the purchase of their home for a reasonable sum. If the Johnsons agreed to the council's offer, then they would purchase the home. Edi said, "If we get it, I think we should tear it down and put in a parking lot for people coming to see the museum. What do you think?"

Opal said, "Let me talk with Sandra and the committee. Personally, I think you are right. If we get a lot of traffic and there is nowhere to park, this will have a negative effect on the residents of Maple Drive."

While Opal was sounding out the committee, Edi made a call to Stan to ask what it would cost to tear the house down and put in a parking lot. Stan thought it was a great idea, and he could keep

costs down. He planned to use a demolition company he knew who
specialized in taking down old homes. They sold the wood, flooring,
and other parts, so their costs were pretty low. He added that one of his
teams could handle the parking lot for a minimal charge. This made
the purchase of the Johnson house a positive move. That was if the
committee was willing. Edi crossed her fingers.

The facade of Edi's old home was all that was left. It graced the front
of the new museum that now covered the entire lot where number 610
had been. The new building was the same gray as the newly painted
shingles on the old cottage. The trim on the windows and doors was
a rich, dark green. The new sign that hung over the cottage facade
announced that this was the World War II Life on the Home Front
Museum. This was the name they had all finally agreed on. The flagpole
stood near the center door, proudly displaying the American flag and the
flag of Indiana. The museum looked stately, impressive, and inviting.
The citizens of Bexley were proud of the new museum and eager to
see what their community had donated. Everyone was talking about
it. There was even a regular feature in the newspaper reporting on the
development of the new addition to their town.

Evidently the *Bexley News* was read by Democratic Representative
Carson and State Senator Kimble. They both had been calling Edi,
wanting to host a grand opening for the new museum. They both said
they would be able to get media coverage to let the whole state and
even the whole of the Midwest know about this exciting new tribute to
Indiana. Edi had politely thanked them and said she would pass their
suggestions on to the Bexley town council and the committee they
had set up to develop the new museum. She knew they would have
to do something about the opening, or these politicos would make it
a media circus. She intended to pass this little task over to Opal and
Sandra. It was just up their alley. They would want to be in charge
of the museum opening and would not want to be overshadowed by
Carson and Kimble.

Later in the week, Mayor Haywood called to tell Edi that he wanted
to have a granite monument erected in front of City Hall. It would
contain all the names of those men and women from Bexley who had
lost their lives in World War II. Edi was surprised when he mentioned
women. The mayor went on to explain, when she asked about this, that
he had found two women from Bexley who had served as nurses in the

Pacific who lost their lives. When Edi went on to say that she did not know there had been any women from their town who had actually served, the Mayor said his mother had known the family of one of the women. Seems both were farm girls who had gone to nursing school and then volunteered to serve overseas. "So I wanted you to know that we will be erecting this memorial, hopefully in time to coincide with the opening of the museum." Edi thanked Mayor Haywood and sat back to reflect on the impact the museum was having on the town and people of Bexley.

"Where do you want me to put these mannequins, Mrs. Harris?"

Edi looked into the truck. "How many of them did you find for me?" she asked. The truck driver said that they had picked up about two dozen of the older types in a store in Indianapolis. "I think that should be enough," Edi said. The truck driver carted the mannequins into the warehouse where they would stay until they were dressed for their roles in the museum exhibits. The idea of having mannequins posing as part of the exhibits was Sandra's. She thought it would add a touch of realism if they had a man seated, listening to an old radio as it played Roosevelt's nightly fireside chat. She had gathered a group of people to help her dress the mannequins and pose them in with the exhibits when these were in place.

With so much going on, it was difficult for Edi to keep track of everything. Elli wasn't of much use as her new home was being framed and she and Stan were busy with it. The whole town seemed to have a heightened awareness. People stopped Edi on the street to ask how things were going and when the museum would be open. Edi knew she had to concentrate on two things: completing the exhibits and putting together a grand opening event.

Just as she was thinking about these two challenges, she got a call from Mary Arnoult. She said she had a friend who worked for Fox News. She had told him about the museum Bexley was building, and he thought it might make a good human interest–type feature for their evening news show. If Edi was interested, she thought her friend could send a reporter to attend their grand opening and add it to their evening news.

This was a gift from above. It solved the problem posed by the two politicos who wanted to turn the opening into a political media circus, and it gave them national coverage! Edi was thrilled and told Mary to tell her friend they would be happy to have them cover their grand opening. Mary assured her she would tell her friend to call Edi to set everything up. It now became imperative that they set a date for the grand opening. Edi called Sandra and told her they needed to have a meeting with Opal and the council to discuss setting a date for the grand opening. She shared the opportunity of having Fox News feature them on nationwide news. Sandra was overjoyed. She promised to get right back to her with a date and time for everyone to meet.

A hastily called meeting of the council took place two days later. After much discussion, it was agreed that the grand opening would be Saturday, May 12, at 7:00 p.m. It would be dark enough for the lights inside the museum and its outside lights to make the museum look imposing and impressive. This date gave everyone involved just enough time to complete the exhibits and even the adjacent parking lot. The council left the meeting excited about the upcoming event. A lot was changing for the good in Bexley.

Edi and Elli had changed their martini time to late afternoon once Stan had become a part of their ritual. The three of them sat in Stan's living room sipping their drinks and discussing all that was happening in Bexley. Stan said, "You ladies have certainly changed this town. It has gone from being a commuter home for Terre Haute and Bloomington to a town in its own right, resplendent with what will be a first-class museum every state would be proud to have. And the town should be proud of you."

Elli leaned over and kissed Stan and said, "That is so sweet of you to say."

Edi smiled and said, "Who would ever have thought, and all this started with my sample social hours and Elli's coming to live with me."

* * *

Now that the interior of the museum was finished, Opal and Sandra's volunteers, who would become the docents for the museum, began to put the displays together. The first one was of a man in suit and tie leaning forward toward an old Philco floor-sized radio. The radio was playing one of FDR's fireside chats. This would be continuously repeated. The next display featured a woman dressed as an auxiliary hospital aide rolling bandages. A little further on was a display paid for by Goodyear Tire Company showing a man in overalls rolling a rubber tire out of large photo of a rubber plant. On the other side of that display, it showed tires being fitted onto trucks and jeeps. The legend put on the display by Goodyear explained how tires manufactured near Bexley were essential to the war effort.

In yet another display, a mannequin dressed as Rosie the Riveter, in a shirt and trousers and wearing a head scarf, was about to add a rivet to the side of a bomber. This display was courtesy of the US Air Force Retirees organization. The legend on the display read, "With grateful thanks to all the Rosies who made our planes the safest to fly against our enemies."

As these displays came together, it became clear that the mannequins were a great asset to the exhibits. They put the human element into each display, making it seem more realistic. Everyone who saw the displays thought the mannequins were an excellent addition. The last display to go in was sponsored by the local churches. The backing of the display was a giant-sized photograph of the old chapel with people streaming up the walkway to the church. In front of this was a pulpit with a man dressed as a minister addressing an imaginary congregation. A recording kept repeating the minister's words, "Let us be thankful this day that the terrible war is over and we may now return to a world at peace."

Opal and Sandra viewed the displays and talked with the docents, urging them to get familiar with the exhibits and displays so they could talk with the visitors knowingly.

Sandra said, "You know, Opal, I get teary-eyed looking at these displays."

Opal nodded and then said, "Look what we have created—of course with the help of Edi."

* * *

It was the middle of April, and spring spread its loving hand over the land. Edi sat in her little space in the Baxter construction offices. She was reviewing what had been done and what still needed doing. She had just sent letters to Carson and Kimble, thanking them for their interest and inviting them to attend the grand opening being covered by Fox News. *There. That ought to cool their jets*, she thought. She had approved the colorful brochures that told about the museum and gave an explanatory tour of it. They had decided not to try and open a gift shop as they didn't want to get into the T-shirt or knickknack business. If there were a lot of requests for souvenirs, they would handle it then. With Opal and Sandra and their docents completing the displays and exhibits, Edi turned her attention to the grand opening.

The opening was set for 7:00 pm. The *Bexley News* was running a front-page article that morning welcoming the people of Bexley to the grand opening that evening. They were reminded that Fox News would be featuring their museum on their evening broadcast. Everyone was urged to come and be part of the event. Edi was sure there would be a large crowd. She had advised the local police to expect this and be actively moving around to prevent any problems.

Chapter 10

Elli had hired two local caterers to set up large tents in the parking lot next to the museum. They would be serving beer, wine, and soft drinks along with snacks of different kinds. This was being sponsored by the local distributors for Coca-Cola and Budweiser.

Edi rubbed her eyes. She was tired and worried that she would forget something important. The phone rang, and it was Elli reminding her that it was martini time at the Baxter house. Edi smiled as she hung up the phone. "Elli is right. It's time to call it a day."

* * *

Flowers were sprouting everywhere, and the lushness that comes to grass, trees, and plants from warm spring rains was gracing Bexley's lawns and gardens. Nowhere was this more evident than in the baskets that hung from the lampposts along the main street of town. Yellows, blues, reds. Pinks and greens nodded gently from the swaying baskets. Children coming home leapt up to try and hit the baskets, but they were a bit too high. It was a gentle time of the year, a pause before the heat of summer and the whirr of lawn mowers.

Stan and Elli stood in front of what was to become their new home. The framing was done, and the siding was going on. Soon they would begin to add the gray shingles that would turn it into the Cape Cod they both wanted. Rick and Bobby wanted to please their dad with how well they handled the daily operations of Baxter Construction. They even had a small crew putting up Edi's cottage. All was going well, and Stan could see they were on time with their plans.

"I will be glad when the grand opening is over so I can concentrate on our house," Elli said.

Stan nodded and added, "I don't think any of us realized all that was involved in developing the museum and involving everyone in the community."

Stan's cell phone rang. He answered it, listened for a minute, and said, "All right, I'll be there in a few minutes."

"What is it Stan?" Elli asked.

"Probably nothing, but it seems the state board of licenses and permits wants to see me at city hall." He kissed Elli and left.

"I wonder what that is all about," Elli said to herself.

"Now, Mr. Baxter, it has been called to our attention that your company has built a museum-type building on land that was only approved for a private residence. This is a violation of State Code 05743302. Unless you have proof in writing that you were granted permission to build a public building on land intended for a private residence, the building must come down and a fine must be paid to the State, the amount to be determined by our department."

Stan was stunned. He distinctly remembered discussing the land ownership with Edi. She had sold the property to him, and he had filed for the necessary permits to erect the museum. He looked at the two men facing him and said, "I will provide you with copies of the documents and permits I have. I would like to know why you are bringing this up now, after the museum has been completed."

"To answer your question, we received a call from an interested party suggesting we look into the ownership of the property."

Stan asked, "May I ask who that party was?"

"I am not at liberty to say, however, you should know that our state legislature and our member of the Senate keep up with affairs here in Bexley as they should."

Stan said he would bring the permits and other documentation he had to them the next day. After he left, he called Edi and told her they needed to meet to discuss this last crisis.

"For heaven's sake!" exclaimed Edi. "With all that we have yet to do to prepare for the grand opening, all we need is the politicians, who seem to have had their feathers bent by being left out, making things hard for us."

Luckily, Stan had kept all the requisite paperwork in a file so he was able to put together what they had asked for. He told Edi not to worry about this. He would take care of it. He said it was more an annoyance than anything else.

The next day, Stan met with the men and showed the permits and documentation he had on file. What made this almost humorous was that one of them had signed the permit!

"Well, we want to thank you for showing us your documentation. You are certainly organized."

Stan smiled, politely thanked them, and with true grace, didn't mention the signature on his permit.

As he left the building, he called Edi on his cell phone and told her not to worry. The problem had been solved. He laughed as he told her one of the men felt a little sheepish when he saw that he had been the one who signed the original permit.

* * *

It was the last week of April, all the exhibits and displays were in place, with the mannequins strategically placed. They were testing the sound system. The selections were such hits as Glenn Miller's "String of Pearls," and songs like, "Don't Sit under the Apple Tree." The idea was to have this music playing softly while the docents answered questions and directed visitors. Edi smiled with satisfaction as she walked through the museum. She took the stairs up to the small theater. She was pleased to note that the music was louder here. They had done this deliberately so the silent movie would have musical accompaniment. Everything was in order. Opal and Sandra were in charge of the docents and had trained them well.

"We are ready to host the opening when all the citizens of Bexley will come streaming through to take a trip down memory lane to what life was like in their fathers' and grandfathers' time." Edi picked up one of the colorful brochures that would be given to visitors as they entered. It featured a few of the displays and told the history of Bexley during the war. As she looked up, she noticed a large clear plastic container on the counter at the entrance. It was filled with the little rubber tire key chains donated by Michelin Tires. *This is not a good idea*, she thought. *People will just grab a handful when they are meant to have just one or two.* She made a note to tell Opal and Sandra to have the docents give them out, one to a person or two to a family. This made them seem more valuable and meaningful.

The sound of pounding hammers and the whine of buzz saws made it hard to talk. Elli and Stan were standing in front of their new home. The builders were finishing the framing, and it was now possible to see the actual shape of the home.

Elli grasped Stan's hand and said, "It is really going to be lovely, just as you designed it in your sketch. I just hope all the selections I have made in rugs, wall colors, and furnishings will be right for our home."

Stan smiled down at her and said, "Remember, I helped you choose, so if something is not right, it will be both our faults. But I wouldn't worry. You have excellent taste, so I am confident our home will be just what we want."

The light was beginning to dim as Stan and Elli made their way back to Stan's house in time to meet with Edi for their evening martini ritual.

Across town, out on the highway leading to Indianapolis, Forest Forsythe was taking a call from Fox News. "No, this airfield can only handle small aircraft and helicopters. The runways are too short for the kind of aircraft you are talking about. Sorry, I would love to accommodate you, but I'm set up to run small hops to Indianapolis, Chicago, and other places within about 250 miles. If your reporters can come in by helicopter, we can work out a deal. Let me know what you want to do."

* * *

Near the end of April, Edi got a call from Harry Randell of Fox News. He wanted to come to Bexley for a preliminary visit to determine what and how the television company would handle the six-minute feature spot on their news program the evening of May 12. He said to Edi, "What I would like to do is walk through the museum to see what camera angles would best showcase the place. I also would like to meet with and talk to you; Stan Baxter, who built the museum; and the two council members who first came up with the idea. Could you set up such a meeting?"

"Of course," Edi replied. "You mentioned this Friday. I think I can get everyone together, and we can do a walk-through as the museum is now complete. What time shall I expect you?"

"I am driving down from Indianapolis and was told that it would take about an hour, so I plan to be there at about ten o'clock."

Edi told him that would be fine. She gave him directions to the museum and told them they would be ready to receive him there at ten o'clock.

Edi called Opal and Sandra and told them of the upcoming meeting with the Fox News man. They were excited to think they were going to be on national television.

Sandra said to Opal, "This is really big. We need to tell our husbands. They are going to be so proud. We also need to make appointments to have our hair done and pick out new dresses for the occasion. Just think, national television! We need to call everyone to make sure that if they are not coming to the grand opening, they are watching it on television. Do you think we should prepare something to say—you know, about how we came up with the idea for the museum?"

"I think we should be prepared. Let's write some notes and practice them. How would it look if the community leadership flubbed on television!"

At about the same time, Edi and Elli were reviewing the plans for the grand opening. The tents, food and beverages were all set. Stan had gotten klieg lights and a rotating beacon to illuminate the front of the museum. The local police planned to be there to ensure the crowd was orderly. Mayor Haywood had agreed to open the ceremony with a few remarks—very few—and turn the event over to Edi and the Fox News announcer. The local newspaper would have their staff reporter for business news there with a photographer to capture the event.

That evening, as they sat in the living room of Stan's house having a martini, Elli asked, "Is there anything we haven't thought of? I am so afraid we are leaving something out. Edi, maybe we should look over your endless lists to make sure we are fully prepared."

Carefully, they went through, page by page, the lists Edi had in her three-ring binder. When they finished, the only item they hadn't done was to decide what they were going to wear. "Since we will be standing under the big American flag and the banner of American flag stripes over the doors of the museum, I think I should wear my red crepe dress, and, Elli, you should wear that bright-blue dress with the boat neckline."

"Red and blue, you know, that is really appropriate, Edi. Those dresses are simple and stylish. OK, that settles that," said Elli. She turned and asked Stan what he was going to wear. He laughed and said that he didn't think that it mattered too much. He said he would wear a navy sports coat and tan slacks and a shirt and tie.

Edi closed her binder. "We have covered everything. I know that there will be something we haven't even thought of that will creep up, but when it does, we will just have to handle it. Stan, you have been a godsend. Without your help, Elli and I would have had a truly difficult time putting all this together."

Elli smiled up at Stan and squeezed his hand. He looked at both of them and said, "I would have helped you anyway, but this little lady who has made my life complete made it a pleasure to be on the team with you."

Chapter 11

Reverend Clarence Wilson, pastor of the Universal Baptist Church, seated himself across the desk from Edi. He smiled at her and said, "Thank you for seeing me. I have been following your efforts to build a wartime museum and bring visitors to our town. I congratulate you on your efforts. Just yesterday, I was made aware of the war memorial being erected outside our town hall. I have a concern that both the memorial and the museum may not properly reflect the involvement of the black community. After all, many of us served in the military, and unfortunately, some never came back. I want your assurance that we will be truly represented."

Edi nodded. "I am so glad you came to see me. We have been very sensitive about this issue. Let me bring you up to date on how we have addressed it. First, the memorial lists all the citizens of Bexley who lost their lives, regardless of race, creed, or color. Second, in putting the exhibits and displays together for the museum, we made sure to include mannequins representing all races and photographs depicting all races working in the war plants as well as in the home. In fact, I think it would be a good idea for you to take a tour of the museum right now with me to ease your concern."

Several hours later as they finished walking through the museum, Reverend Wilson was pleased with what he saw. "You have done a really fine job of representing all aspects of our community. This is a museum we can all be proud of."

Edi smiled and said, "I am glad you approve. I just had a wonderful idea. As you know the grand opening is going to be on national television.

I think it would be very appropriate if you could be there wearing your military uniform. You could join Elli and me and say a few words about how our new museum reflects all aspects of our community. What do you think of the idea?"

The reverend stood a bit straighter as he replied, "Why, I think that would be a good idea. I know my congregation will be pleased to see their pastor in the opening ceremony. Thank you for wanting to include me."

"That is settled then. Fox News wants all participants in the opening to be in front of the museum by four o'clock. So please plan to be there dressed in your uniform at that time."

The reverend rose from his chair and reached across to shake Edi's hand. "I am looking forward to this event. The museum has already made a major impact on Bexley. I can assure you I will spread the word to my congregation." And so another potential problem had been averted by following Henry's advice. He had told Edie to always ask yourself these questions: who needs to know or be involved, what do they need to know, when should you tell them, where should they get this information, and most importantly, why. She had a faraway look in her eyes as she remembered him saying this. Edi thought of how valuable Henry's advice was.

* * *

Harry Randell's car came to a stop in front of the museum. He got out and stood looking at the front of the building.

Stan walked up to him, "Mr. Randell?"

Harry nodded and reached over to shake Stan's hand. "Yes, I am Harry Randell. Your museum looks very impressive. It should show up very well on camera. Since my time is limited, here's what I would like to do. I want to do a walk-through of the interior and look for the best places for the cameramen to place themselves. With just six minutes, we want to focus on the most interesting locations."

Stan introduced Edi and Elli to Harry, explaining to him that they were responsible for developing the museum. In addition, he introduced Opal and Sandra, telling him they had conceived of the concept. He told Harry that in addition to these four women, they would have a retired army sergeant in uniform representing those who fought. When

Harry asked if the sergeant was really needed, as it might crowd the front of the venue, Stan explained that he also represented the black community. Harry nodded.

He followed Edi and Elli into the building, his eyes sweeping left and right as he took in the space. He stopped a number of times as they went through. He climbed to the small theater and asked to view the film. Once he had seen everything, he came back out and asked if there was some place they could sit down and have a cup of coffee as they discussed how Fox News would like to handle their six-minute human interest feature.

Once seated in the café, Harry took over the conversation. "First, let me say I am very impressed with your museum. It is a unique tribute to all the home fronts there were in our nation. It is going to film very well. We will start out with me standing in front of the museum. The camera will pan up to show the name of the museum and its facade. Then I will introduce the four women and the sergeant. I am sorry but there will be no time for anyone to say anything. I want each of the people being filmed to smile and nod when I introduce them. At that point, I will lead the camera into the museum. We will let the camera pan down and across the aisles to show how you used mannequins to create a warm, intimate, and compelling atmosphere. I will make commentary about some of the displays as I walk through. I will guide the camera up to the small theater and mention the film of life in the 1940s. As we end, we will go silent for several seconds so we can capture the background music. Then we will fade out with the camera focusing on the display of the chapel with the minister celebrating the end of the war. Questions or comments?"

Stan was first to speak. "It sounds very good to me. I like the idea of using all the time you have to showcase the museum interior."

Opal said, "Well, I can understand that time is very tight. Sandra and I had prepared some notes of what we would say. Since there isn't time for this, perhaps you might like to use them. They might give you some ideas for your commentary."

Harry took their notes and thanked them. "Any other comments or questions?"

"Just one, what time will you and your crew be setting up, and is there anything you need from us to help you?" Edi asked this as she opened her binder to take down any requests he had.

"I can't think of anything else for now. Just so you know, we have rented a helicopter to carry us and our gear. We will be landing at Forsythe Field around noon, giving us plenty of time to set up our cables and cameras. If there are no other questions, let me give each of you my card. If something comes up, call me, and either I or my assistant will get with you."

After Harry Randell had left, the rest of them stayed in the café, going over what he had explained to them. Opal was the first to voice her comments. "I am disappointed that we won't be able to say a few words, I mean, it will look like we didn't have much to do with building the museum. But I can see, if every one of us said a few words, there wouldn't be any time left for him to show the museum." They all nodded.

Edi opened her binder and jotted down a note. "I had better call Mayor Haywood to tell him that he won't be able to introduce everyone—in fact, he really doesn't need to be there. I am sure he will be very disappointed, but we do want the time spent showing off our museum."

"Is there anything else for us to discuss?" Stan said. "I am asking because I need to get back to the office, and you, my dear, need to check on how the house is coming along." Everyone pushed back from the table and soon were on their way.

* * *

The end of April proved the old cliché "April showers bring May flowers." It rained almost every day, which was fine for the gardens but bad for the golfers itching to get out on the course. Since all the work still needing to be done in preparation for the opening ceremony was taking place inside, the rain only proved a distraction for those wanting to go from one place to another. The month ended with a violent thunderstorm and winds strong enough to cause some restaurant and store marquees to blow down. Power was out for several hours in town. There was flooding in some outlying areas, one of which was Forrest Forsythe's airfield. Forrest waded into his hangar to check his planes. His real worry was that the field would not be dry enough for the television crew to land the helicopter they had rented. Would two weeks be enough time to dry it out?

* * *

May brought sunshine, sunshine, and more sunshine, and with it the beginning of the upcoming summer's heat. Everything dried out. Even the flowers in their baskets along the main streets began to droop. The airfield had dried cracks in the ground—so much for soggy landings. When Edi tried out the air conditioning in the museum, she found that it didn't work. She called Herbert Refrigeration, the company that installed the units, and told them of the problem. "I need you to come over and see what's wrong with the air conditioning. It won't come on. What do you mean, you can't come until next week? I don't think you understand. This is the new museum which has its grand opening in twelve days. We will have national television coverage, and if the air conditioning isn't working and it is still hot, it will absolutely ruin the opening. Now you get over here right now. I don't care if you have to do it yourself, Mr. Herbert, just get it done right away." There was some mumbling on the phone, and when Edi hung up, she was satisfied they would be over that afternoon to make the necessary repairs.

Stan and Elli were in Chicago attending the Building Owners and Manager's Association Conference. BOMA's members discussed what was going on in their businesses and what they could do to help their cities and towns improve and maintain their buildings. Stan thought Elli would enjoy some of the events set up for the women and get to know some of his friends outside of Bexley. They would be gone three days. While they were gone, Edi invited the Baxter boys and their wives to join her for the afternoon martini ritual. For three days, she hosted cocktail parties, which were enjoyed by all of the Baxter family, especially the wives who usually were homebound with their children.

Allison Baxter, Bobby's wife, said she thought they should have something at the museum that would involve young children with the exhibits and displays. She offered to put together a children's treasure hunt leaflet they could use to find different items in the displays. Edi thought this would be a welcome addition and encouraged Allison to design it.

* * *

The three days flew by. Stan and Elli were back. The early heat of summer had people fanning their faces and watering their lawns in the late afternoons. The air conditioning was fixed in the museum, much to Edi's relief. Elli had increased the amount of soft drinks that would be available at the food and beverage tents in the parking lot. She was told to increase the amount of beer too. All of a sudden, it was May 10. That is just what happens. You get busy doing other things, and *bam!* the thing you had been planning for over weeks and months was upon you. That's life. Anyway, time was up. In two days, Fox News would be flying in and setting up their cables and cameras. Harry Randell would be introducing America to Bexley, Indiana, and the wonderful new museum they had crafted. In six minutes, the show would be over. The newspeople would leave, and the people of Bexley would finally be able to see for themselves their new home front museum.

For just a second, Edi wondered if it had been worth all the effort the community had put into it. Then she mentally shook her head. Of course, it had been. They had put Bexley on the Indiana map, even the national map. They had given their town something to be proud of, and they had set in motion the opportunity for future business growth with new restaurants, shops, and perhaps, a heritage hotel. Nothing but good could come from this.

"Who do we know at Fox News? What do you mean they aren't very supportive of our kind of politics? The Democrats run this country! Get me someone high up on that network. I want our Indiana senator and congressman to have a role in this little news feature coming out of Bexley."

And so the wires were burning between the politicians, the news network, and Bexley's mayor and town council. If ever you want to mess up something, ask a politician to help out.

When Stan, Elli and Edi heard about the pressure the politicians were putting on Fox News, they were worried that the news network would get disgusted with the intrusion and decide that the six-minute feature wasn't worth the aggravation and cancel the feature. Stan said, "I know I would, if I were them. They have a great many other events they could use besides us. Is there anything we can do?"

"I think the network is very experienced in handling situations like this. I'll bet they have fobbed off Carson and Kimble on to some guy who will string them along and then lose them at the last minute. We should give the network credit. They deal with politicians all the time. That's their business." After Edi made this comment, the others nodded with a look of some relief on their faces.

* * *

The morning of May 12 was cloudy. *Oh no*, thought Elli, *please don't let it rain today. After all the work and planning, all we need is rain to truly dampen the opening ceremony.* Stan called the national weather station and learned that a front had passed during the night, but by noon it should be sunny and bright. Elli relaxed and called Edi to tell her the weather news. By noon, all the parties were dressed and on their way.

Reverend Wilson had a bit of trouble fitting into his old sergeant's uniform. His wife helped by moving the buttons an inch. It was still tight, but if he stood straight and didn't try to sit down, he would be all right. "I didn't realize I had gained so much weight," the reverend said.

"Honey, you were a lean, handsome soldier when I married you, and that's the way I still see you," his wife declared, smiling at him as she patted his chest.

Everyone was eager for the event to begin. Edi, Elli, and Stan were dropped off and went into the museum to check that everything was in order and the air conditioning was working. Stan looked over the landscaping his sons had completed, and it looked fine. They had added a border of spring flowers, which added color to the walkway. By one o'clock, Reverend Wilson appeared, walking rather rigidly and very erect in his uniform.

Suddenly, it was two o'clock, and Harry Randell and his crew drove up in a rented van. They had flown in by helicopter. As his crew began their setup, Harry ushered everyone to the front of the museum. He positioned them in the places he wanted them to take for the filming. "Please remember, we don't have time for any comments, just smile and nod when I introduce each of you. You all look very good." And with that, he left them to position his cameramen inside the museum.

"I am getting so excited," said Opal. "I think I will go into the café across the street to cool off. I don't want my dress sticking to me during the filming!"

"I will join you," said Sandra. "Anyone else want to get a cold drink?"

Stan and Elli went with them. Edi felt she should stay in case Mr. Randell needed something. Reverend Wilson decided to join them as his uniform was getting exceedingly warm. He couldn't sit down, but at least the air conditioning would ease the perspiration that was trickling down his back.

Edi went in to the museum and found Harry pointing out locations to his cameramen. He paused when he saw Edi. "Is there something?" he asked.

"Yes, I have a question for you. I know that Congressman Carson and Senator Kimble were putting pressure on your network to be featured in this event. How was this resolved?"

Harry nodded as he replied. "This happens quite often. Politicos are always looking for a way to get in front of the public. In this case, the CEO of Fox News called each of them to thank them for their interest and complimented them on identifying the newsworthiness of the feature. He also sent each a letter of appreciation already framed for their offices. So it is all taken care of."

Edi said, "I am so glad. I just didn't want them to spoil the opening by making it a political circus. I will just get out of your way now."

By four o'clock, the network crews were finished. Cables and wires snaked across the sidewalk and over the curb to the van where the camera feed would be picked up and transmitted to the network. Everything was being tested, and so far, so good.

Harry Randell and his crew were taking a break. Everyone was crowded in the café. Harry was reviewing his notes as he sipped his coffee. One of his sound guys came in to tell him that the sound check was clear. He nodded and looked up. "Set up the makeup girl in back of the van. I want everyone who will be on camera to have her check your makeup so you don't have a shine on camera. Ladies, please go to the van and see her now."

Opal, Sandra, Elli, and Edi left to do this. Harry smiled and added, "Gentlemen, this means you too." For the next half hour, they were powdered and touched up.

Sandra said to Opal, "I am glad we aren't going to have to say anything. I will be just too nervous to do anything more than smile." Opal nodded in agreement.

A table was set up in front of the café, and sandwiches, salads, and fruit were made available to everyone. Except for the film crew, most of the food went untouched. Everyone else were too excited to eat.

Harry disappeared into the museum, where he could be seen timing himself as he went through what he was going to say.

Chapter 12

It was about a half hour before the ceremony was to start when the trouble began. People were milling about across from the museum. The police were keeping everyone in line and away from the cameras and lights. The chief of police, Edward Kinsky, made his way up to Stan and the others. "We have a problem," he said. "A group of protesters are coming down Magazine. We can't stop them so long as it is a peaceful protest. We will cordon them off, but we can't halt their protest."

Harry had come out of the building. He said, "We have had this happen before. Here's what we are going to do. We will shoot everything from inside the museum. Have all the participants move into the building. I will position them and do the introductions from there. We will continue the filming as if this was the way we had planned it."

Everyone moved quickly across and inside the building. Sounds of the protesters could be heard as they continued down the street. The crowd in front of the museum could hear them chanting, "Glorify the war no more! Glorify the war no more!"

Edi looked at Stan and said, "What are they angry about? We aren't in favor of war, we are honoring the people who supported and defended our country during wartime."

Stan patted Edi's shoulder and said, "They just want to make trouble. For all we know, they aren't even Bexley citizens, but as often happens in these situations, people bused in for the benefit of the politicians and the media. I am going to ask Captain Kinsky if he knows any more about them."

"A few of the protesters have been arrested for breaking through the line and attacking one of our policemen. It's clear that these people are from out of town. We still can't stop them from demonstrating, but we can prevent them from coming onto this part of Magazine," the chief said.

"Well, that's something, at least. Who instigates these demonstrations, I'd like to know," asked Elli.

Harry answered her. "From our experience, it is usually politically motivated. In this case, I would guess the political forces weren't satisfied with the actions of Fox News' CEO and decided to gum up this opening ceremony with a demonstration to show their political clout. No matter by doing the entire feature from inside they have actually given us a bit more time to show off the museum."

While the chanting could still be dimly heard, it was more of a mumble like the crowd outside were talking. Harry assured everyone that once they started, the noise wouldn't be heard at all.

Just then, one of the policemen hurried in and said that some of the protesters had broken through the cordon and were looting some of the stores. Rocks had been thrown, and one policeman had been hurt in the melee. He said he was told to keep them up to date. Harry said, "This has changed how I will open the segment."

"This is news I have to include in my piece. Unfortunately, we can't afford to ignore what is going on outside the museum. I will keep it short and use it to point out that it makes this museum even more important. I will emphasize that liberty and our way of democracy are truly what this museum is all about, and anyone who is against this is against America."

Time seemed to leap forward. Suddenly, it was five minutes to seven. The crowd of local citizens strained against the police tape preventing them from crossing the street. The protesters were reduced to a few angry, shouting demonstrators. Most of their effort was now ineffectual.

Police Captain Kinsky strode into the museum to let them know the looting was stopped, the damage to property was minimal, and the arrested individuals were on their way to jail. He ended by saying, "I am keeping some officers on the street to prevent any further disruption. Sorry this happened, but it seems like it is happening more and more."

Harry thanked the captain for his prompt and effectual handling of the disruptive situation. "It has almost become a common occurrence in every media event. We now plan contingencies so we can work around these kind of disturbances."

Just then, the lights came on, and the cameraman gave the signal that they were on the air, live. Harry raised his eyes so he was looking directly into the camera as he said, "Welcome to Bexley, Indiana, home of a unique, truly one-of-a-kind museum honoring those who fought the Second World War at home. With me are the Bexley citizens who came up with the idea and made it a reality. Meet Opal Webster, Sandra Richter, Edith Harris, Elli Baxter, and her husband, Stan Baxter. Also here as a reminder of those who fought this war is Sergeant Clarence Wilson. As we walk around this salute to our home front, notice that the exhibits and displays illustrate the many actions the people at home were involved in."

As the camera panned the exhibits, Harry pointed out how the mannequins helped bring the enlarged photographs to life. He pointed out the second-floor theater where a home movie of life in the 1940s played every half hour. After talking the audience through the museum, he paused at the last exhibit showing people streaming into the church. A minister posed at a pulpit was heard saying the war had ended and now there would be peace. Harry paused so the audience could hear the soft music playing songs of that era. He ended saying, "Thanks for joining me at this homage to our past, to those years that changed the world forever."

The camera lights went out, and Harry joined the others. "Mr. Randell, that was so moving. You really did our museum justice. I just hope someone taped it so I can watch it again and again. Maybe we should offer copies of it for sale in the museum. What do you all think?" Edi asked this as she wiped her eyes with a Kleenex.

"I am sure the network will give you permission, so long as you give them credit for the tape. While our crew reviews and makes dubs of the tape, let's go outside and join the festivities," said Harry.

People streamed into the museum. There were exclamations as they recognized things from their past. Fingers pointed and laughs were heard as the crowd made their way through the displays. They pointed out items to each other and paused to read who had donated them.

People were quiet when they came to the last exhibit, which was the 1940 Ford up on blocks. They read the card attached and were silent. Many waited patiently to go up to the theater to view the film of their town in the 1940s. Most were eager to see if their parents or even they had been captured by the film.

Outside, Elli's teams were kept busy providing snacks, soft drinks, and beer to the burgeoning crowd. It was a lively scene. Stan came over to see if he could be of any help to Elli. She was flushed, and her apron was covered in beer stains.

Stan laughed as he hugged her. "How can I help you?" he asked.

Elli used her arm to wipe the perspiration off her face. She gratefully gave Stan the task of pouring the beer while she handled the soft drinks. Several helpers from Budweiser Brewery and several caterers were kept busy handing out hot dogs and bags of different kinds of chips. It seemed all of Bexley had shown up for the grand opening. Edi was gratified but a little overwhelmed by the magnitude of the crowd. She didn't know there were this many people in Bexley!

As night fell, the Fox News team packed up their gear and loaded their van in preparation for heading back to Forsythe Field and their waiting helicopter. Harry thanked everyone for their participation and assured them that it was a success. Then, with minimal fanfare, the news crew left.

The crowds began to wane. Families left to put their children to bed. The docents looked exhausted. They slowly started picking up dropped leaflets, brochures, someone's shoe, and a rain poncho that was still in its wrapper. It had previously been agreed that the museum would be closed the day after the opening ceremony to give the maintenance staff time to clean up. Everyone was thankful they had made that decision.

"Come on, let's hear some feedback from the people who went through the museum and from anyone who saw the Fox News feature," said Stan. He spoke up first. "Everyone I talked to said the opening was great and the museum terrific. They even commented on how well the police took care of the agitators."

"I heard the same thing from the people I asked. One thing I heard over and over was how the mannequins made the displays seem real. I think we scored a hit," said Opal.

Sandra chimed in, saying, "I heard the same thing. I also heard them saying they were proud that their town was on national television."

Elli said, "Well, all I know is they ate us literally out of everything. If it hadn't been for Stan, I would have drowned in beer. So as far as I'm concerned, it was a real success."

Finally, Edi entered the conversation. "I spoke with the Bexley news reporter who was taking notes for the morning paper. He said he heard nothing but accolades from everyone. They said they loved the museum, especially the 1940s film of the town. They wanted a tape of the television feature since they didn't get a chance to see it. Most can't wait to read the paper tomorrow. I know we are all exhausted, but we should be really proud of the job we have done. We certainly put Bexley in the news. Thank all of you for the efforts you made to make this such a success. Of course, we have only begun, but the major work is behind us."

The morning newspaper's front page contained pictures and articles reporting on the opening ceremony events. The headline said BEXLEY MUSEUM SCORES A HIT. Readers had to look several pages back for an article reporting on the demonstrators who tried to spoil the opening. This proved that their efforts had been unsuccessful, more of an annoyance than anything.

Edi was having coffee with Elli and Stan. They had eagerly awaited the paper and pored over the pictures and articles. Finally, Stan looked at Elli and said, "Now I hope we can focus on finishing our home and let Edi handle running the museum."

Just then the phone rang. It was Opal and Sandra. They were literally gushing over the articles in the paper. "We are just thrilled with the praise our museum and the opening got in the paper. We have decided to host a celebration cocktail party at Sandra's home this Friday. Plan to come and join us. You know, if you hadn't turned our original idea into reality, none of this would have happened. So come and expect to receive lots of accolades!"

Elli answered, saying, "What a great idea. Please be sure to invite the docents who bravely managed the crowds within the museum. Also, it would be a very good idea to invite Reverend Wilson, as he was part of the ceremony. I know you will have someone from the *Bexley News* there, and they will be sure to include his attendance in their coverage of your fete."

"My, what helpful suggestions. We will be sure to include everyone you mentioned. I don't know why we hadn't thought of them to begin with. Thanks so much. We are still on cloud nine, and we haven't even viewed the tape of the Fox News feature. I thought we could have that running at the party. What do you think?"

"What a terrific idea. I am sitting here with Edi and Stan, and they are nodding in agreement. We all are looking forward to your party. Thank you for thinking of doing this. We certainly need to celebrate, and since you both always host the best parties, this one is bound to be a success."

After Opal hung up, she turned to Sandra and said, "They are excited about our hosting the party. You know, we need to talk to our husbands about how to turn this to their advantage. Edi is going to need someone to advise her on how to manage the maintenance, insurance, bills, and income that will come from the museum. It should be one of our husbands."

Sandra smiled and said, "Of course."

* * *

Garbage trucks, street sweepers, and the street water truck were busy putting Bexley back to normal. The parking lot tents had been taken down and the beer kegs removed by Budweiser. Hosing the parking lot was about to begin. Everyone who was part of the cleanup was cheerful. They had been part of last night's crowd and had enjoyed themselves, so cleaning up was not so much of a chore.

Cleanup was also going on inside the museum. The maintenance crew was vacuuming and dusting and washing counters. They cleaned the bathrooms and finally bagged all the trash and took it away. By midafternoon, everything was back to normal.

The Tennetti Brothers, who had been given the job of moving the facade from Edi's home and installing it to the front of the museum, were standing across the street, viewing the building. Pete said, "Well, we may not have renovated the old house, but we built something much better and more important."

"Yah, every time we drive down Magazine Street, past this museum, we can take credit for completing Bexley's first-class museum. How about that, huh?"

Pete smiled and nodded. They got into their truck, and as they drove slowly away, he said, "It was our lucky day when those ladies called us in to see if we could help them."

* * *

The next day the museum had reopened. Quite a number of people came to view the displays again. Some went up to see the film as the crowds the day before had prevented everyone from viewing it. Opal had wisely gotten additional volunteers trained as docents, so they helped on this first real day of business.

For the next few weeks, Mayor Haywood received calls from the mayors of cities and towns across the Midwest. They had viewed the Fox News feature and were impressed. The mayor always gave credit to Edi and the others, but secretly he liked the idea that his fellow mayors thought he was responsible for putting his town on the map with the new museum.

Throughout the rest of the spring and summer, tourists stopped to see the new museum. Edi was kept busy managing it. With the council's help, she set up a museum board, chaired by Ralph Webster. Sam Richter took over as financial advisor for the museum to help Edi. Both sides benefited from this arrangement. Edi got good advice so she could make good decisions, and Sam and Ralph enhanced their reputation in Bexley. This was advantageous to their personal business. It was, as we hear people say, "a win for everybody."

Friday night came, and it seemed as if Opal and Sandra had included the entire town in their celebratory party. Guests strolled from the bar area to the dining room, where they ate their fill of all the delicious foods found in steaming chafing dishes. They had erected an easel with a sign pointing the way to the viewing room where the Fox News feature was playing continuously. Edi, Elli, and Stan were stopped repeatedly by well-wishers. It took them quite a while, but at last they made their way to the patio area outside.

"What a wonderful party. Opal and Sandra have outdone themselves. I appreciate all the kind words, but to tell you the truth, I am a bit worried." Edi said this as she fanned herself with a museum brochure.

Both Elli and Stan looked a bit dumbfounded, and finally, Elli asked, "What are you worried about? Everything has gone so well."

"Yes, that is true so far as it goes. But this reminds me of movie stars and celebrities. I once heard Bette Davis say in an interview that it is very hard to stay on top. She said she was only as good as her last movie."

"What has that got to do with what we have accomplished for our town?" Stan asked this with a frown on his face.

"Well, once the initial enthusiasm and excitement wear off, people will start wondering what is going to happen next. It may become a game of 'Can you top this?' Or people will get back to their daily lives, and the museum could die a very slow death, dependent on tourists to keep it going. This will work during the summer, but once school starts, those tourists will slow down to a trickle. That is what I am talking about."

Stan nodded. "I see what you mean. You know, I have an idea. Why don't we talk with the school administration and offer them a big discount if they will bring their students who are studying World War II to the museum. We would be doing a community service and keeping the museum in the public eye."

Edi nodded. She said she thought that was a good idea. Elli suggested they get the *Bexley News* to do a feature once a month on one of the displays, complete with pictures. They all agreed that these were good ideas.

Then Stan said, "Looking forward a year from now, we might want to host a one-year anniversary and let the politicians get involved. If they take part, it will mean media coverage, because they don't do anything without having it covered by the press and the media. They can fight over who takes credit for helping Bexley create a unique museum that reflects the patriotism of this great state." Stan said the last part of this with a bit of a theatrical flourish. The others laughed.

Then Elli said, "I think we should discuss all of this with Opal and Sandra. They might have some other ideas, and I am positive they want the museum to continue to succeed. After all, now that their husbands are involved, they have even more at stake."

It was time to go back inside and join the party. Some people had left, so the noise level had diminished. Some of the waiters were refilling the chafing dishes, but fewer people were filling their plates. It looked like most of the action was around the bar. Stan got his back slapped by a few of his golfing buddies, and some of the ladies who had been at the bar several times were giving hugs and air kisses to Edi and Elli. The video of the Fox News feature was a great success. Opal came up to Edi and told her they had made a copy for Edi and one for Elli.

"As usual, you have hosted a wonderful party. This was a great way to end the opening of the museum," Edi said. She and Elli were making their way to the door with Stan leading the way.

"Sandra and I were happy to host this, and we are thrilled that our original idea has turned into something that will benefit our town for years to come. Opal and I are so proud of what all of us have accomplished." Once again she hugged Edi and Elli.

As they made it through the front door, Stan said, "I get a kick out of those two. They may have had a fuzzy concept, but without your planning and organizing which made it all a reality, it would have either ended as an idea or even a disaster."

Edi shook her head. "They made significant contributions, selecting and training the docents, hosting endless coffee hours to publicize the museum, getting their husbands involved in the financing and management of it. No, they have been valuable helpers in this whole endeavor."

Stan said, "You are right. I seem to have ignored all their efforts."

* * *

Through the rest of May and into the summer there was a steady flow of tourists to Bexley and the museum. Edi was kept busy managing the daily activities and handling the many phone calls from people wanting information about Bexley, where it was, and the museum. She finally had the docents take over the phones.

As was typical during the summer, there were a number of thunderstorms that rolled across Indiana. Near the end of June, Stan, Elli, and Edi were just sitting down having their afternoon martini when the phone rang. Stan answered it. "What! Where did it happen? Is there anything I can do? Of course, I'll be right over."

Elli was first to ask the question. "What has happened?"

Stan was already heading toward the door. He stopped, turned and said, "Glen Harper got hit by a bolt of lightning on the golf course. EMS said he died of a heart attack caused by the lightning strike. They asked me to come over to handle the crowd of golfers that are milling around and to help with phone calls."

"How terrible! Glen was such a nice man. I think he has three small children and a wife who teaches at the middle school," remarked Elli. "I wonder if anyone has thought about going over to his house to console his wife. I don't know her well enough, or I would go. I think I will call Stan on his cell and ask him to have someone go over, if they haven't already."

By the time Stan got to the country club, they had taken Glen away. He had gotten Elli's call and acted upon her suggestion. Glen's best friend, Marty Schoen, had been on the course with him. He had gotten out of the rainstorm minutes before the lightning hit. He was sitting with his head in his hands, dazed with grief over the loss of his good friend. Stan asked him if someone had gone over to Glen's house to be with his wife. Marty looked up and said nothing. Stan repeated his question, and Marty shook his head as if to clear it and answered, "Oh my god. Of course, I should go. He was my best friend, and Anne needs my support right now. I will go."

"Do you want anyone to come with you, Marty?" Stan asked this with concern in his voice.

"No, I need to do this, but thank you, Stan."

And with that, Marty left for his car. Stan watched him go and then turned back to the other golfers and told them that unless they had a reason to stay, the course was closed for the day. The rain had wiped out all the games, and the tragic death had hit everyone hard.

Chapter 13

June turned into July. While Glen Harper's death had made an impact, like most human events, it had faded away from people's minds. The whirr of lawn mowers, the sound of sprinklers, and the smell of sweet grass together with the sight of kids riding up and down the streets of Bexley brought things back to normal.

Several tour buses were parked in the parking lot. The drivers were sitting in their air conditioning as their passengers enjoyed taking a tour of the museum. A number of them were snapping pictures of the front of the building. Edi had been gratified when the tour companies had begun making the museum a stop on their Indiana tours. She was in her little office in the front of the building when a man poked his head through her door and asked if she was the museum administrator.

"Yes, I am. How can I help you?"

As he came into the room, he explained, "I have just been through your museum and am quite impressed. It came to me that every state was a home front during the war, yet as far as I know, Indiana is the only state to create a museum honoring its participation in the war. I work for PBS, and if it is all right with you, I would like to talk with them to see if they might have an interest in doing a documentary on how this museum came about."

Edi was taken aback. Such an idea had never occurred to her. Once she had composed herself, she said, "Well, I would have to talk with the museum's board, but I don't see any harm in having you pursue this with your company. If there is truly an interest, we can schedule a meeting with all involved and take it from there."

"My name is Charles Davis. Here is my card. I didn't get your name."

Edi took his card and gave him one of hers. "I am sorry. I am Edith Harris. How long do you plan on being in town?"

Charles pocketed her card and said, "Only for a short while. I am on one of the tour buses. I have found these buses a great way to get a feel for our country. I will give you a call in a week or so and let you know if there is any interest." With that, he left to rejoin his tour. Edi sat there for a few minutes, trying to grasp what had just gone on.

Later that afternoon, while she, Elli, and Stan were having their martinis, she told them about the visitor from PBS.

"Wow! Wouldn't that be something!" exclaimed Elli.

Even Stan was enthusiastic about the idea. Edi, ever the cautious one, reminded them that it was a three-minute conversation and would probably amount to nothing.

Before they moved on to talk about the new home being built, Stan said, "You never know what might happen."

Elli and Stan's home was almost complete. The team was working on the interior. Stan had also hired a landscaping company to come in and landscape the grounds around the house as well as the grounds leading up to the pond. Edi's cottage was complete. She had taken a few days off to move her things into the cottage. She had had the builders make her ceiling-to-floor bookshelves like she had had in her cottage. Now she lovingly put Henry's bits and pieces from his trips onto the shelves. She added their old favorite books. Once the furniture was in place and her clothes were in the drawers and closets, she sat down at her kitchen table and looked out at the pond. It was peaceful and quiet. She said to herself, "Henry would have liked this place. I know he is happy for me. I just wish I didn't miss him so."

The summer's heat bore down on everything and everyone. People took to watering in the evening when it had cooled down. People walking on the sidewalks had to be careful to avoid getting drenched by the sprinklers in everyone's yard. It was a typical summer in Bexley. Everyone remarked that they couldn't remember a summer as hot as this one, but then they said that every summer at about this time. The pastors and priests, as they did every year, asked people to increase their giving to help pay for air conditioning in the churches. But, as in every year, whatever they collected seemed to be needed for other things.

As July moved toward August, Edi received a call from Charles Davis. She was surprised to hear from him, thinking that nothing would come from the brief conversation she had had with him. He said, "I have discussed your town and the home front museum you have built with the producers at PBS. There is sufficient interest for us to make an exploratory trip to your town. This doesn't mean we will do a special feature. It means we will come and explore the possibility. Are you still interested?"

Edi felt a surge of excitement. She forced herself to calm down, and thought, *This still doesn't mean anything will come of their visit.* "Yes, we are interested. When will you be coming to see us?"

"In that case, we plan to fly in to Indianapolis this Friday. We will drive down that day and spend the weekend getting a take on the town and the home front museum. If we think the concept is viable, we will set a date for our team to come and do the feature."

Edi asked what he needed from her. "Your confirmation that you and anyone else you think we should meet will be available that weekend and that we will have your assistance in our review of your town."

"You will have that," Edi said. "I can also suggest that you stay at the Old Coach Inn. It is very close and has excellent accommodations and food." She gave Charles the phone number for the inn, and they ended their call with Charles promising to call when they arrived in Indianapolis.

Edi started one of her lists. She needed to let the mayor know that PBS was coming to consider doing a feature on the town and the museum. She also needed to give a heads-up to the Old Coach Inn, the museum board, Stan, Elli, Opal and Sandra, and Harold Kinsky in case the local police needed to assist in any way. She added a call to the town landscaping crew to spruce up the flower baskets and flower borders and water down the streets the day before that weekend. There were probably a number of other things she probably needed to add to the list, but at that moment, she couldn't think of any. The only thing that was top of her mind was that PBS was coming. She leaned back in her chair and stared at the poster of the museum on her office wall and took a mental trip down memory lane.

She thought of how everything started with her visits with the sample salespeople. Then there was the arrival of Elli and their martini hours with different contractors. Their request for a visit with Baxter Construction led to Stan and Elli falling in love, which of course led to their wedding. Then there was the opening ceremony for the museum with the involvement of the whole community. She didn't want to forget the drama of the Fox News coverage of that opening. It really was a lot to take in. Now the possibility of a feature on PBS. The only dark cloud in all of this was the death of Glen Harper. His wife Anne and their three children were being supported by their many friends. It was a good thing that Anne had this time to spend with her children before school started in the fall.

While Edi was ruminating over the past, Elli and Stan were concentrating on the present as they put the finishing touches to their new home. Anyone passing by would see a beautiful Cape Cod with dove gray shingles, white-framed windows and a cherry-red front door. It was warm and inviting. Every time Elli walked up the front walk, she fell in love with it all over again. The landscaping Stan had ordered was complete, and it looked as if the house had been there for years.

The first call Edi made was to Elli. "You aren't going to believe who I just talked to—PBS! They called because they want to make an exploratory visit to see if they want to do a feature on our town and museum for their *Sunday Morning* program. Can you believe it? Tell Stan. We can talk about it more this afternoon over a martini. See you then!"

Edi decided to wait until she talked with Elli and Stan before making any more calls. She could just imagine that if she told anyone else, they would spread the word all over town, and that might spoil their opportunity to be on PBS.

That evening, after hearing the news, Stan said, "The fewer people who know about this, the better. We want them to see our town and the museum as it is, without the interference of the mayor, the town council, the museum board, and the locals who will want to try to get into any feature they might do."

"You are so right, Stan. For now let's keep it to ourselves and decide jointly who else needs to know. After all, Mr. Davis and his producers might decide that we aren't that newsworthy, and that could be embarrassing for everyone. I am so glad I didn't make any of the calls I had on my list. Thank goodness I waited until I talked with you two," said Edi.

Friday loomed, hot and muggy. Edi sat by the phone in her office, waiting to hear from Charles Davis. He had told her they were landing at about noon and would be out as soon as they picked up their rental car. Edi estimated that they would be in Bexley by three o'clock, so the heat of the day will have abated. She had asked the gardening crew to make an extra pass around the flowers in front of the museum.

Edi was excited, but she didn't want to show it. She wanted to act professional and calm. She planned to take them on a personal tour of the exhibits and displays as she explained how the museum came to be. She would keep her comments brief to encourage them to ask questions. Once they had viewed the museum, she would call Stan, who would take them around the town and finally to their rooms at the Old Coach Inn.

Before she knew it, it was two thirty, and Charles Davis was walking into her office. "Well, we made excellent time." He moved over to introduce the two producers who had accompanied him to Bexley. "Mrs. Harris, meet Mary Clayton and Donald Weil, coproducers of *PBS Sunday Morning.*"

"It is very nice to have you visit us. We are very proud of our town and the museum we created. I hope you find it interesting and newsworthy. Let me take you on a tour of the museum."

"Before we do that, we'd like to learn a bit about how the museum came to be. What was the impetus for building it, and what has been the impact on the town of Bexley?" As Charles made this comment, he and the producers arranged themselves around Edi's desk and took out a small tape recorder with which to capture her remarks. For the next half hour, Edi gave them a synopsis of the history of the museum, ending with it being featured on Fox News during their opening ceremony.

"Is that enough background for you?" Edi asked. She had been aware of the tape recorder and had tried to speak clearly and succinctly. Now she looked at her visitors to see if anyone had a question for her.

"Thank you for this overview. It gives us a context from which to view the museum. So if you will, let's take that tour now. We will use the recorder as we go along to record our comments to help us later when we discuss the museum. Is that all right?"

Edi said yes and proceeded to lead them into the museum, stopping at each display and exhibit to explain their use of mannequins to personalize and add a touch of reality. She pointed out how each related to the efforts put forth by the people on the home front. She also gave them several pauses to hear the music of the 1940s playing softly. They ascended to the small theater and sat for the film of Bexley in the 1940s. Coming down again, they stopped to look at the 1940 Ford car up on blocks.

It was four thirty when they had finished the tour. Edi was so tense she was worried that her voice was going to start quivering. Just as they came back to her office, Charles said to her, "That was a very thorough look at your town's idea of what life was like on the home front. Thank you so much for taking the time to take us around personally."

"It was my pleasure. We are very proud of what we have created here. One thing I should tell you is that once school has started, we will be hosting those classes studying the war so they can observe firsthand what the people at home had been doing to support the men who fought for all of us."

The PBS staff met Stan in front of the museum. He took them on a tour of Bexley, stopping at the war memorial in front of town hall. When he stopped at the Old Coach Inn, he played a tape of the Fox News feature for them. He felt they had gotten a good look at Bexley.

Edi flopped into her chair and started breathing normally again. She hoped she had done the museum justice. They had asked quite a few questions, which meant, to her, that they were listening and interested. She hadn't had a chance to read their reactions as she was too busy trying to concentrate on what she needed to say. It was five o'clock, and she called Elli to tell her she was on her way over and to please have a drink ready for her; it had been a taxing day.

Edi was glad they hadn't told anyone about the PBS visit. After a few days had passed, she put it out of her mind and went back to managing the museum and greeting the visitors who continued to come through on these summer days. Things were going well.

* * *

Stan and Elli had finished the decorating, and their home was complete. They especially loved sitting on the patio and looking out over the pond to the woods beyond. At night, if they were lucky, they could even count the stars above. Stan had decided to buy a telescope so they could get a better view of them. Their house was just what they both had envisioned. Down, nearer the pond they could see Edi's cottage. Her lights had just come on, meaning it was martini time in the Baxter household.

Stan said, "I don't care if PBS comes or not. Even without them, I think we have done a lot to help Bexley improve. We have built up community pride, created a meaningful legacy with the museum, and even added a few new shops and at least one new restaurant. I can honestly say, we have made Bexley a better place." Elli and Edi both nodded in agreement.

The Baxter household wasn't the only one in town that was enjoying the advent of evening. Down Maple Drive, Opal, Sandra, and their husbands were having their own refreshments. Sam Richter handed the ladies their old-fashioneds and then poured a scotch and water for Ralph.

Sam said, "I don't know if you girls have heard the latest—it seems that we may be having another big event here in the near future."

"What are you talking about?" Sandra asked as she put her glass down. Opal smiled and nodded at her husband to continue. It seems she already knew where the conversation was headed.

"Well, one of the maintenance crew happened to hear Edi talking to some people from PBS. According to what he could gather, they are considering doing a piece on Bexley and the museum for one of their Sunday morning programs. Now, that would be something for you girls to get involved in. We just might use that to our advantage. It is good business to be able to tell potential clients about how we are helping our town."

* * *

"Good afternoon, Bexley Home Front Museum. How may I help you?" The docent handling the phone responded to the caller, telling them that Mrs. Harris was not available, but that she would get the message. Later, when Edi had returned, the she found a message on her desk. It read, "Mr. Davis will call you this afternoon."

Edi sat down. This was the call they had been waiting for. She tried not to get her hopes up, because she didn't want to be disappointed. She got busy going over the financial statement for the month of July. It had been a good month; they had made a decent profit. She thought that it was partly because of the tour buses. Her real concern was how would they do when school started and people were no longer traveling.

The phone rang. Her mouth went dry. She answered, saying, "Home Front Museum. This is Edith Harris. How may I help you?"

"Hello, Edith. It's Charles Davis. We wanted to get back to you about our idea for showcasing your town and museum on the *PBS Sunday Morning Hour*. After reviewing the recordings we made and the notes we took of the museum and the town, we think it would be a good fit for us. Our plan is to air the piece the first weekend in September. This will mean we will have an advance team arriving next week to begin layouts for the video shoot. How does that sound to you?"

Edith tried to control her excitement. "That sounds just fine. We are very glad you want to use us on your program. May I ask, about how long do you think our segment will be?"

"At this stage, I can only give you an approximate time. I think it should be about ten minutes. We will start by viewing the town and then focus in on the museum. I can give you a better idea once our team has completed their design and layout. I will call you in a few days to tell you who will be coming and exactly when."

Once they had hung up, Edi took a deep breath and called Elli. "PBS just called. They intend to do a ten-minute piece on our town and the museum!" "I know, I am so excited. Tell Stan. For now, we had better keep it to ourselves, or everyone will want to be in it."

Then Edi got a call from Opal. "I heard from a little bird that we may be having a big event coming up. Is that true? You know you can trust Sandra and me. We want to offer our services in any way you need us—oh, and our husbands too."

Edi asked, "What big event are you talking about?"

Opal replied, "Well, Ralph heard it from a reliable source that PBS is going to do a feature on our town and our museum."

Edi pressed her lips together and replied, "I don't know if that is going to happen or not. It is still up in the air. I will let you know when I know, Opal."

"Well, as they say, the cat is out of the bag. Opal called to ask me about the big event with PBS. I stalled her, but it won't be long before we will have to make it public knowledge." She said this as Stan and Elli had come down to see her completed cottage. They were seated around her kitchen table, when Edi brought up this bomb. Stan shook his head and wondered out loud who had been giving out this news. It had to have been someone in the maintenance crew, he thought. He made a mental note to talk with his sons about this problem.

In a few weeks, PBS would be filming in the town. This meant that there would be a lot of speculation as to who was doing the filming and what it was going to be used for. Stan suggested they get the *Bexley News* to do a spread on the upcoming PBS program so everyone got the same information and there was no need for rumors to run all over town.

Edi picked up on this and had a talk with the paper's editor. He agreed to cover the upcoming event in their next Sunday newspaper.

* * *

The hot weather continued, but down on the pond, it was much cooler. Stan had decided that he and Elli ought to go on a little vacation while they had the time. He booked reservations to Saint Bart's, and they flew off for a week on the island.

Saint Bart's is a lovely island in the Caribbean. They had a luxurious thatched hut with a ceiling that pulled back, revealing the nighttime stars. Elli lay on the bed, exclaiming it was absolutely breathtaking. She had spent the whole day in the water, trying to catch the dolphins they had in a pool. Stan laughed as she squealed when one came close. As Elli wrote on her card to Edi, it was an absolute paradise, and if she could, she would never leave.

Just as all good things must come to an end, Elli and Stan came back, brown from the tropical sun and sorry that their second honeymoon was over.

It was a good thing that they had come back, because the town was all over itself trying to think of ways to insinuate themselves into the upcoming PBS filming.

One benefit of all the excitement was that people started to spruce up their homes and lawns. They wanted to be sure that if they were in the film, they would look good. So there was a minor frenzy of painting, landscaping, and window washing. Bexley never looked so clean and tidy.

Naturally, the mayor and the town council wanted a slice of this pie. Mayor Haywood felt it was his place to welcome the PBS people to town and host them in a dinner. He and the town council also thought it would be a good idea if the council held a mock meeting in which they recreated coming up with the idea for the museum. And of course, the museum board would be included in this scene.

Edi graciously accepted all these suggestions and told everyone she would pass them on the producers, but that it was up to them to decide what they wanted to include in their feature. She told Charles Davis of the high interest and learned that he was not surprised. "This happens every time we come into a community to do a feature. Just thank everyone for their interest and ignore the suggestions."

A week had passed and the film crew arrived. They had taken rooms in the Old Coach Inn and during the first few days were barely noticed by the people in town. They filmed early and by midafternoon were in their van, editing. But by that weekend, things heated up. They began filming in the streets and in front of the buildings on Magazine Street. It was hard to ignore them.

"I feel like I am in Hollywood," trilled Missy Dunn. "Isn't this exciting!" she exclaimed to her friends as they arched their backs, trying to look out the window of the coffee shop.

Stan ended up being the go-between for the film crew and the town. He helped plan where they would be filming and got some of his people to make sure the area was cleared for the crew. PBS appreciated his support and let him know it.

"There is one challenge we are really going to need your help with," said Charles as he and Stan sat in Stan's living room. "During the feature, as we view the town, we want it to look like it normally would.

That is we want people walking down the streets, going in and out of shops and stores. It won't make a good feature if the streets are empty."

"I see what you mean. I think we are going to need to have a call for people who want to be extras in the feature. But I am not sure how to do this. What have you done in other places you have filmed?" Stan asked.

"The simplest way is to place a notice in the paper saying we are holding auditions this Friday in the town hall. We will be selecting thirty-five men, women, and children over five. If interested, be at town hall at nine o'clock, Friday morning. Your job will be to corral the crowd and keep it orderly," said Charles.

Stan shook his head. "It could be a riot, you know, a bunch of milling people all eager to be on television. I can see some pushing and arguing over who was there first. Do you think I should have the police there?"

"It won't be that bad. We have done this before. Here's what happens. As soon as the doors open and people start coming in, we start 'walking the line.' Our staff walks through the line of people, selecting who they want. Within thirty minutes, we have made our selection. We thank everyone for coming and ask those selected to stay for instructions. Then our team gets names, addresses, and phone numbers of the ones chosen. A cameraman takes quick shots of each person so we know who we will be looking for during the shoot. We will pay each person used in the actual filming one hundred dollars.

"Hey, I am doing all this work for you for nothing. What's the deal?" Stan said, laughing. "I don't expect anything, I am just joking."

Charles laughed and replied, "You get our appreciation and acknowledgement in the feature's credits."

Chapter 14

The day of the auditions, Stan was not surprised to see a large crowd milling around town hall. Most of them had dressed up. Some were wearing hats and coats even though the weather was hot and sticky. At precisely nine o'clock, Charles Davis opened the doors and asked for everyone's attention. The crowd surged forward a bit and grew silent to listen. He said, "Thank you all for coming. We will ask you to come through the doors one by one, except if you have brought a child, in which case, would the mother or father accompany their child? As you go through, if selected, you will be asked to stay, and someone will escort you to the extras' room. If you are not selected you have our thanks for coming. Now, if the line will begin passing through."

Stan watched as his friends and neighbors straightened up and walked forward, eager to be selected. In about twenty minutes, Charles stopped the line and told those still waiting that they had completed their selection. He thanked those waiting and saw that each of them received a small tote bag with DVDs of PBS shows as a way of easing their disappointment.

The group that had been selected were busy congratulating each other, sure that each of them had that special something that would look good on television. Charles Davis came in and asked them to be seated. He said, "Once we get started, you may be sorry you were selected." There were genial smiles and nods, as if they were old hands at this business. Charles continued, "We will be asking you to be available the week we are filming, which is set for the second week in August. We will give you instructions on what to wear, and you will need to wear this each day during the shoot. You will spend a lot of time just waiting around until you are called to the set. Most of what you will be doing will be walking up or down the street, going into and out of stores, or waiting to cross the street. You will not have any lines to say. You are what we call background filler, used to make the scenes more realistic. Now, if any of you can't be available that week, or if you have decided you would rather not participate, that is fine. Just let the crew member with the clipboard by the door know, and she will take you off our list."

Two men got up and went to the door. They explained they couldn't be off work that long. Everyone else stayed. In a few minutes, Charles had the cameraman taking their pictures, his crew getting each person to sign their network contracts and verifying names, addresses, and phone numbers. It was an active and busy scene.

Elli and Edi wanted to hear all about the auditions. Stan said it was surprising to see how organized and efficient the PBS crew was in keeping the townspeople in check. He said, "Even some of the women you would expect would raise a commotion over not being picked were mollified by the calm way the crew thanked them for being gracious in coming as they gave them their tote filled with DVDs of PBS shows."

"Were Opal and Sandra there?" Edi was interested in whether the girls wanted a moment of television immortality.

Before Stan would answer, Elli said, "I doubt if they would ever consider themselves extras in anything." Both Edi and Stan laughed. "That is very true. Watch, I will bet they are going to host one of their famous cocktail parties for the PBS crew, and they won't take no from Charles and his team." Elli said this nodding sagely.

Wouldn't you know, Stan got a call from Sam Richter, Sandra's husband the next day. "Say, listen, Stan, the girls want to throw a party to host our PBS friends. We're thinking this Saturday might be a good time. Think you can run that past them and let us know if the date's all right?"

"Sure, Sam. I will ask them and get back to you." Stan put the phone down and remembered what Elli had said. She sure was right. He then called Charles. When Charles answered, Stan said, "Now, don't kill the messenger, but two of our esteemed socialites want to throw you and your crew a cocktail party this Saturday evening. I can promise you fabulous food, lots to drink, and quite a few people who will gush all over you. What shall I tell them?"

There was some laughter on the phone. Finally, Charles said, "Don't worry you are too valuable to kill. Tell them we would be delighted, but we can only stay for an hour as we have a lot yet to do. You can give them an extra thrill—tell them Carl Rhodes, the host of *PBS Sunday Morning*, will be here this weekend and will attend also."

"That will put them over the moon. I will let them know, Charles." Stan called Sam back and relayed the news.

Sam could hardly wait to hang up so he could call his wife. "Honey, we have scored a coup. Carl Rhodes, the host of *PBS Sunday Morning* will be here, and Charles Davis says he will bring him to the party. You and Opal better get cracking. This has to be your best party yet!"

Out beyond the center of town, there were a lot of small ranch houses occupying an acre or two. On most there was a chicken coop, a vegetable garden and maybe a cow or a horse. These were the people who drove the garbage trucks and picked up the trash. They also drove the water trucks and did the maintenance jobs for the town and the townspeople. They had not been a part of the museum's opening ceremony other than to clean the streets and build the parking lot. They were also not part of the excitement over the upcoming PBS show. Even though they worked to prepare for all these events, they had not felt invited to participate in them other than to watch them on television. It was just not their world. They were not part of the community Stan talked about.

That's why when Charles Davis came looking for his niece, Peggy Davis, they were surprised. Here they had a relative of a television producer living in their midst and didn't even know it. Evidently, she didn't either, because when she answered the door, she was looking at a stranger. Charles introduced himself and said he had promised his mother he would look Peggy up. They had a nice visit, and he invited her to take part in the filming. Naturally, that got around, and pretty soon, all the people living in Bexley Acres were making plans to come and see Peggy getting filmed. That is how the *whole* community finally got involved in the next big event, the filming of *PBS Sunday Morning*.

PBS had asked Stan to bring together the parties who wanted to know what the PBS feature would say about the town. When everyone, including Mayor Haywood, was seated in town hall, Charles explained that the PBS show would begin as always, with Carl seated, facing the camera. He would make his introductory remarks explaining that they were about to visit Bexley, Indiana—a small town typical of all small towns across America except for its unique salute to American life on the home front during World War II. He would go on to briefly tell about the museum, and then he would turn from the camera and face a screen showing Magazine Street. The camera would pan down the street. It would pause to show Peggy smiling as she watered a flower box in front of the coffee shop. It would move on to show people walking, going into the stores, and crossing the street. Carl, now acting as narrator, would tell the viewing audience about the town and the museum, which would then be in view. The doors to the museum would open, and the camera would move inside. Carl Rhodes would tell the viewers what they were seeing as they viewed the displays and exhibits. He would pause so the viewers could hear the music softly playing. The segment would end with Carl reminding the audience that every town in America had been a home front, but only Bexley, Indiana, had chosen to commemorate it.

Everyone was pleased. The mayor cleared his throat and said, "I think this will be a fine tribute to our town. Call on me if there is anything you need—police coverage, anything."

Charles Davis smiled and said, "I am glad you approve, Mayor. Are there any questions I can answer?" When no one spoke up, he continued, "In that case, I had better get back to work. If you think of anything, let Stan know, and he will get with me."

That evening Stan was off working with his sons on some construction issues, so Elli and Edi were having their martini ritual alone. "I am just overwhelmed by what PBS is planning to do. It almost makes me want to cry. I am so proud of all that we have accomplished, aren't you?"

"I certainly am. And I think we should be proud. Just look at the differences we have made in Bexley. One thing to our credit is we haven't gone around tooting our horns. We have kept a low profile, as we should have."

They were sitting in the living room of Edi's cottage. Outside, they could hear crickets and see flying insects trying to fly into the patio lights. It was a peaceful place. After Elli had gone, Edi prepared for bed. Once under the covers, she thought of Henry and mentally kissed him good night. As she fell asleep, she thought of how he would be so pleased at the way everything was turning out.

* * *

"Mrs. Webster, where do you want these cheese puffs to go. The tables are all pretty full." Opal patted the back of her chignon and directed the caterer to an area for the puffs. Sandra was rearranging the large floral display for the third time, which meant she was getting nervous. Their husbands were consulting with the bartenders and having their first drink of the night.

Just then, the doorbell rang, and Frances, Opal's maid, answered the door. It was the beginning of a steady stream of people, all dressed up and ready to party. At nine o'clock, Stan, Elli, and Edi arrived. They were accompanying Carl Rhodes and the rest of the PBS team. Sandra and Opal rushed up to greet their guests of honor.

"We are so happy to meet you. We watch your shows all the time. We are so looking forward to what you will be doing with our little town."

Sandra ran out of breath, and Opal picked up for her. "I am just thrilled to have you here. Let me introduce you to my husband, Ralph Webster and Sandra's better half, Sam Richter."

Carl Rhodes, used to being a celebrity, smiled graciously and thanked them for hosting this cocktail party for him and his team. He moved into the room, greeting people as they came up to him and accepting their compliments. To the hosts and hostesses, the party was a success. Everyone was mingling, and the conversations flowed throughout the room and out unto the back patio. Carl Rhodes and his team were on the patio, away from the crowd.

"I think they have taken enough pictures with us and we have met most of the guests. I think it is time we made our exit. I will lead the way. Try not to stop too many times for more conversation. If any of us do that, we will never get out of here," Carl said.

He passed back into the dining room and made his way to the front door. He graciously thanked people and took many pats on the back as people tried to make it look like they were friends of his. His team had less trouble and they all made it to the front door without a hitch. Stan got a signal from Carl that they were ready to leave. Stan went out and got the town car he had waiting pull up so the PBS team could get in and drive off to the Old Coach Inn for the night.

Even though the main attraction had left, the party continued for several hours, during which Ralph and Sam worked the room, trying to drum up clients. Opal and Sandra kept the caterer busy refilling platters while their husbands moved over to the drinks table and made sure that everyone's glasses were refilled promptly. It was a busy scene. Edi and Elli gave Stan a nod meaning they were ready to leave. He nodded and went out to get his car. On the way home, Edi remarked, "I think it was a very successful party. Mr. Rhodes was certainly gracious and patient with all the questions people asked and all the pictures they took!"

"I am just glad it is over," said Elli. "Now all we have to worry about is the day of the filming. I am praying for sunshine. Wouldn't it be terrible if it rained that day?"

"I am sure they are used to having weather challenges. They probably have some contingencies to work around that if it happens," said Stan. He was driving home when his cell phone rang. He handed it to Elli and told her to take the call.

"Hello? Oh hi, Sam. Yes, we thought it was a real success too. Please give Opal and Sandra our thanks for hosting such a great party. Yes, tell her we will call her tomorrow to talk about our involvement in the PBS filming. Goodbye, Sam."

* * *

As usually happens in the Midwest in summer, the heavens opened and sent down lots of rain. Local people call these rainstorms "gully washers" because they cause rain to fill up the streets and people to create water waves trying to drive through. And that was what was happening the week leading up to the filming. Then, lo and behold, the skies turned bright blue, and puffy clouds raced across the town. Everyone was so thankful because it meant the filming could take place as planned.

Once they had filmed Carl Rhodes's introductory segment and were ready to open up the filming of the town, there was a lot of noise as four local boys came down the street on their motorcycles. Harold Kinsky, who was there to protect the PBS people, ran out on the street and stopped the bikers. He had several officers take the boys into custody for disturbing the peace. Later he would tell Stan that they just wanted to be on television. Typical kids.

From that point on, the filming went well. Carl became the narrator as the camera filmed the town, first showing Peggy Davis smiling as she watered her flower box. It panned down the street so the audience could see the local people stopping at a light and then crossing the street. It followed others as they made their way down the street, some entering stores, others coming out of them. It looked like a typical small town on a typical summer's day. The filming paused at the front of the museum as Carl told the listening audience the significance of the museum they were about to view. With his narration continuing, the viewing audience entered the museum. Carl explained what they were seeing. He took them through the displays and exhibits and paused at one or two, allowing the music of the '40s to be heard softly playing in the background. Once he had come to the 1940 Ford up on blocks, he ended his narration, giving credit to the town of Bexley for honoring their home front. As he completed his narration, the film paused and took the audience back to a final view of the town.

When the initial filming was complete, they did several retakes, filming the street again and asking the people to replicate their actions. This took the rest of the day, but as the light began to fade, they called a halt. The filming was complete. Now they would turn their attention to editing. Stan was told that they would show the completed feature to those involved in the filming sometime in late August. Since the feature was set for the *PBS Sunday Morning Show* the first week of September, they were right on schedule.

* * *

During the summer, time seems to go slowly, especially in small towns where there isn't a lot to do and the most exciting thing is going to the Dairy Queen or the air-conditioned movies at night. During the days, parents let their children run through the sprinklers to cool off. Most children in Bexley ride their bikes out to the pond at the end of Maple Drive. They leave their bikes at the edge of the woods and play games until it gets dark. Everyone sits on their front porches or back patios and fans themselves. They watch the fireflies and listen to the crickets singing in the trees. It is peaceful, hometown America.

This summer was no different for most of Bexley's townspeople. Edi, Elli and Stan were sitting on Stan's patio, taking turns viewing the stars through the new telescope Stan had bought. "I didn't know there were so many stars in the sky," exclaimed Elli as she gazed through the telescope.

It was August, the beginning of what is called the dog days of summer. Edi was kept busy by the tourists visiting the museum. The coffee shop across Magazine Street had gotten approval to set up a soft drink and snow cone stand, and both were doing great business serving museum visitors.

Stan kept in touch with Charles Davis. He expected the PBS people to return at the end of the month to give them a preview of the upcoming PBS program that would air the first week in September. There was an undercurrent of anticipation in the town as everyone awaited the show. Even the people out in Bexley Acres were eager to see their own Peggy Davis on the TV.

They held the preview at the Bexley Cinema so there would be enough room for everyone to attend. Stan, Edi, Elli, and both Opal and Sandra viewed it ahead of time and were very excited by how the town looked and how well Carl Rhodes did in highlighting both the town and the museum. "He paid us many compliments for honoring the home fronts of America and made our town out to be a great place to live," said Edi.

"I can't wait to hear what everyone else has to say," said Elli.

The doors opened, and the crowd moved in and took their seats. It was interesting to see the mixture of people as those from Bexley Acres mingled with those living in town and on Maple Drive. As soon as everyone was seated, the lights dimmed, and the preview started with Charles welcoming them and saying that PBS was pleased with the feature and he hoped they would be too. He ended by saying he thought it was one of the best PBS had done. There was a hush, and the preview began. It was only ten minutes in length, but for those ten minutes, not a sound was heard from the audience. They were mesmerized by seeing their town on the screen. When Peggy Davis was seen watering the flowers and smiling, a few people nodded smiling. When it was over, there was loud clapping, and many were asking if they could see it again. Charles showed it again. As people left the movie house, you could hear them talking excitedly to each other. They were proud and happy to live in Bexley.

Chapter 15

Mayor Haywood was in Indianapolis, attending the annual Indiana Mayor's Conference. This was an opportunity for the mayors of the state to get together and share what they were doing to help reduce crime and improve living conditions in their towns. A lot of good ideas were generated during the conference. While it was very beneficial, it was also a time for the mayors to brag about what was happening in their towns. Usually Mayor Haywood, who had attended several of these events, didn't have a great deal to say. However, he was really looking forward to this year's conference. For once he had something to say to show off his town.

Saturday morning, Mayor Haywood asked for fifteen minutes of speaking time and the use of the large screen and video player. Once he was introduced, he told his fellow mayors about the building of the Home Front Museum and the subsequent Fox News segment showcasing it. He went on to talk about the tourist buses stopping in Bexley and the increase in new businesses. He ended by telling them about the September *PBS Sunday Morning* program featuring Bexley. He reminded them that the museum honors those who supported the war from home. He asked them to watch as they previewed the upcoming PBS special. Charles Davis had let him take the preview film to show the other mayors. Mayor Haywood turned on the video player and sat back proudly to watch along with the other mayors.

When it was over, there was a break for coffee. He was congratulated by many of his peers, many of whom said they were going to come and see the museum themselves. All in all, it was a great conference for him.

He felt he had done his town proud. As he drove home, he couldn't wait to tell the town council.

There were more than just mayors at the conference. Several reporters were also in attendance. One of them had attended Mayor Haywood's presentation. He reported on it and the upcoming PBS program for his paper, the *Indianapolis Gazette*. This was read by all the Indiana politicos. Each party wanted to make hay out of it. The question was how to turn it to their advantage? One thing in their favor was the fact that the program would not air until the first week in September, so they had some time to let Indiana and even all of the Midwest know how they had been the driving force behind PBS seeing the value in the Life on the Home Front museum and the town of Bexley. They got their media people busy crafting the wording and preparing to make TV spots they could use on local news programs. As usual, whenever politicians and the media get involved, you can bet it will turn into something like the three blind men trying to explain what an elephant is.

Mayor Haywood was gratified that his presentation had made the news. As he said to himself, "I sure put Bexley on the Indiana map." When he entered town hall that Monday, he got several pats on the back.

It wasn't long before all the excitement had died down. People went back to life as usual. They went to work, came home, and sat on the porch and had a cool drink while the ceiling fan circled overhead. And as usual, Edi, Elli, and Stan had their martinis and caught up on what they had done that day. They were looking forward to the PBS special, but it wasn't their whole world. Stan was planning a trip to England. Edi had promised herself a week at the Heritage Resort and Spa in Northern California. She had dreamed of going there, and now she intended to make it happen.

Stan turned on the evening news just in time to catch their democratic state senator being interviewed by one of the media news pundits. He was saying that he had been working tirelessly in the senate to get funding to help in the building of the Bexley museum, and it was rewarding to see his efforts succeed. Stan laughed out loud. He said to Elli, "I can't think of one thing the Indiana state senate did to build or promote our museum. What nonsense. I hope everyone will realize this is just the politicians trying to mix in for their own benefit."

Elli responded, "They may not believe him here, but that may not be true for the rest of the state. After all, they don't know what really took place. Also, this goes out to the whole Midwest, so he may find more receptivity than you would expect."

"You are right. It is not just the state senate we have to consider, it is also the state legislature. Representative Carson is sure to try the same tactic. It might be a good idea for the *Bexley News* to do a piece cataloguing the events that took place leading up to the museum and the television news segments. They could share this with papers across the state. What do you think?"

Elli thought for a minute, then answered, "It is certainly a worthwhile step. I also think we might think about doing some sort of telephone campaign. We all know people all over the state that we could call to refute the politician's assertions. I'll bet Opal and Sandra could set up some sort of telephone marathon. We get them involved, and believe me, the politicians won't know what hit them!"

"Why don't you and Edi have lunch with them and see what they think of your idea? Remind them that this is just the first round of these media spots by our politicians."

Edi, Elli, Opal, and Sandra met for lunch at the Trellis Tea Room. They had not seen the media spot with the senator. But they were not surprised. "It really irks me that our politicians are trying to take credit for what we created. We have decided when election time comes up, we are going to host lots of campaign parties for their opponents," said Opal. Sandra nodded in agreement and added, "When I think of all the donations we collected and how our community came together to turn our concept into reality, I am resentful and insulted by the senator's media spot. I know there will be more, and the legislative representative will get in on the action too."

The four ladies discussed what could be done to reduce the effectiveness of the politicians. "One thing we might do is get the editor of the *Bexley News* to contact his fellow news editors across the state. He could tell them that there are no facts supporting the senator's and legislator's statements. He could tell them to disregard their news spots," Sandra suggested.

"That's an idea. Which one of us would be the best person to take this on?" asked Edi. Everyone looked at her. Edi said, "OK, I will do this and let you know my results by the end of the week. What else can we think of?"

"Well, there's that program called *Indiana Today*. We could see if we could have some time on it to share what Bexley has done to promote tourism and enhance our state's reputation. Since one of the program's news anchors was in my sorority at Indiana State, I could call her and see if they would be interested," said Opal.

"Could you do that this week? We want to nip any more of these news spots in the bud," suggested Elli.

Opal agreed. They paused to consider other actions they might take. More iced tea was ordered, and the ladies discussed upcoming vacations. The Websters were going to Hawaii. Edi shared her plans to go to the Heritage Resort in California. Elli said they were planning to visit England. There was just enough time to go before the end of August. Sandra said they were going to Nova Scotia to the Keltic Lodge and eat the world's best scallops.

Elli watched as one of the tearoom staff finished cleaning the front window and went out to clean the other side. She looked at her friends and said, "You know, sometimes you have to go outside and then come back in again. You have to think outside the box. What about creating a diversion that will take the politicians' minds off Bexley and give them something to worry about."

"What do you have in mind, Elli?" Edi seemed intrigued by her friend's idea.

Elli continued, "I was thinking, no politician wants to have his name in the news for being sued for lying to the public. There are a number of attorneys who we know and are friends with. I am sure we can get one of them to represent the town of Bexley versus our esteemed senator and state legislator for false representation. We can get the *Bexley News* to publicize the lawsuits. I'll bet the attorney will even work pro bono for us. This should distract them, at least until after the September PBS broadcast."

"Who has the best attorney contacts? We need to do this right away," said Elli. She looked at the others, waiting for a volunteer.

"I will take this on. I know several attorneys, friends of my husband. I will ask him which one I should approach. I will get this done, including the contact, by the end of the week," said Sandra.

At this point, they had run out of ideas and iced tea. Edi said she would check with each of them during the week to see how they were doing. She also told them that they would share their plans with Stan, and if he had any other ideas, she would share them with everyone. They left the tearoom feeling as if they had at least taken some action to squelch and make an end run around the politicians.

The next day, there was another political spot, this time from the state representative. He smiled as he told the viewers that Indiana should be pleased that their representative was actively involved in making Indiana well-known in the Midwest because of the Bexley museum that he had been instrumental in developing. This just increased the feeling of the urgency for what they had to do.

Elli told Stan how they had decided to block the media spots. She was surprised by his reaction. "I don't know if those spots are so important, Elli. Most people don't pay much attention to the politicians. The only ones who listen are not the ones who pay the bills or vote. My guess is if we ignore them, they will fade away, especially once the September broadcast is over."

Elli shared Stan's comments with Edi and the others. "You know, he makes sense, but I still don't like sitting still while they take credit for doing nothing," said Opal. "I say let's go ahead and get everything ready, but hold off initiating anything for two weeks. If we want to go ahead at that time, we will pull the plug then. Everyone agree?" They all agreed.

The two weeks went by without any noticeable reaction to the politician's media spots. Once more, Stan was right. Edi was kept busy by a steady stream of visitors to the museum. Elli and Stan planned their trip to England, a place that Elli had always wanted to see. She told Stan she wanted to see Buckingham Palace and the Tower of London. Elli sent off for her passport, excited by the idea of becoming a world traveler. She got busy planning for the trip.

Edi decided that she would go to the Heritage House Inn and Spa for her vacation. She booked her flight to San Francisco and rented a car to drive to the Mendocino resort. She was lucky to get a cabin at the inn, as it was busy at that time of the year. So it looked like the Baxters would be in England and Edi would be in California as the summer ended and the town settled down, waiting to see themselves on the PBS show.

* * *

It was a hot, muggy evening, Edi, Elli, and Stan were having a martini before having dinner. Edi had brought over some spare ribs she had fixed, and Elli had made a salad, so they could afford to wait a bit. Stan turned on the news. He wanted to hear the results of the tennis match going on at Wimbledon. "I'll turn this off as soon as I find out who won today's match," he said. After hearing the results, he was about to turn off the television when Elli asked him to turn to the news to see what had happened that day. On one of their local news programs, they heard the announcer say, "State Senator Paul Kimble has resigned from the Indiana Senate where he served three terms. He was partly responsible for the passage of the state highway bill and the development of the Bexley World War II Museum. He cited personal reasons for his resignation."

Stan turned the television off. He turned to the girls and said, "I wonder what is going on. Just recently his people were beginning to work on his next election campaign. When I hear the phrase *personal reasons*, I think something shady is going on."

Edi put down her martini glass and looking at Stan said, "Well, it could be he is ill or someone in his family is ill. You remember a few years ago when one of the state representatives, Nancy Russo I think, resigned to care for her husband who had cancer. She cited personal reasons when she left."

"If there is something behind this, it will surface soon," said Stan. "In the meantime, we have our own plans to make. Edi, when do you leave for California?"

"I fly out to California on Monday. I think by then the attendance at the museum will have begun to slow down, with school starting and less tourists coming. I will be gone a week. I am really looking forward to this trip—I have heard wonderful things about Heritage House," Edi said.

"We are leaving next week too," Elli said.

"Yes, we are staying at Brown's Hotel in Mayfair," added Stan. "Elli hopes to catch a glimpse of the royal family," he added.

Elli blushed and said, "I admit, I have a crush on the royal family. Just being there will be enough of a thrill for me." Edi and Stan laughed.

It stayed hot and muggy, even on the golf course. Several members were in the pro shop, looking at the clubs and asking Coach Brown for his opinion. "Get up on the practice mat and take a few swings with each club, see which one feels comfortable," he said.

The door opened, and Stan came in. He had just finished his round and wanted to cool off in the air conditioning of the pro shop. "Hi, Coach. How's it going? Your suggestion that I widen my stance when I putt has really paid off. Thanks."

"Good. I need a cold one. Let's move over to the grill. Hey, Dicky, take over, I'm going over to the clubhouse with these guys. Be back in an hour," Coach said.

When everyone was seated in the clubhouse bar, Stan said, "I heard that Senator Kimble resigned. He said for personal reasons. Any of you know anything about that?"

After the others shook their heads, Coach said, "I heard a couple of people casually talking about him. Seems he was pressured into it, something about money changing hands if he could get Charles Davis to interview the Governor and let him introduce the PBS broadcast."

"Oh, for crying out loud! He doesn't have any clout with the newspeople. His media spots are pitiful. No one pays any attention to them. What is it? Are all our politicians worthless, or am I being too harsh?" Stan said.

"Yah, they are a sad bunch. Having him resign isn't much of a loss, would you say?" asked the coach. Everyone laughed in agreement.

* * *

As summer continued, Edi was gratified that it had been a profitable month for the museum. They were in the black and had a surplus to tide them over as fall began. She had trained one of the docents to take her place for the time she would be away, so she knew the museum would be in good hands. Edi had never traveled alone before and was a little apprehensive about her trip. She thought of all the trips Henry had taken to far off, remote places; surely she could take this trip in her own country. "I will just have to screw up my courage. The worst that can happen is I get lost and have to ask for directions," she said out loud.

As the PBS show would air the first Sunday in September, Opal and Ralph decided to have a dinner before everyone left on vacation. They invited Edi, Elli, Stan, and Sandra and Sam. At the last minute, they added Stan's sons and their wives, as Bobby and Rick had been instrumental in building the museum. It was a lively group at the dinner. There many toasts to the success of their endeavors. It was a time to blow off a little of the pent-up steam they had accumulated, waiting for the upcoming Sunday show date.

Once home, Elli hugged Stan and said, "Thank goodness we have you on our team. Your levelheadedness and common sense kept us on the right track."

Stan smiled and kissed her on the forehead before replying, "Thank you, my dear, but everyone contributed to our success. I am just glad I got to be a part of it."

* * *

Edi's flight to San Francisco was uneventful. She pulled her bag to the car-rental desks and got the keys to a modest little sedan. She had the car-rental people outline what roads she should take to Heritage Resort. With the route outlined in red, Edi went out to her car. She left the airport with one hand on the steering wheel and one hand holding the map. She didn't realize how tense she was until she noticed the moisture on her hand was getting the map damp.

"Get a grip. For heaven's sake, once you leave the parking lot and turn left on Highway 1, it is a straight shot," she said aloud.

Soon after, she was driving down the highway out of the city, across the Golden Gate Bridge and through Sausalito. It wasn't long before the highway was banked on both sides by giant redwoods. Every now and then, she caught a glimpse of the Pacific. It was really beautiful country. The road began to curve and dip up and down, so Edi paid careful attention. The woman at the rental desk had told her that Heritage Resort was in a dip in the road, off to the left. It was a few minutes later that she saw the small sign saying "Heritage House." She turned into the drive and followed the road a hundred yards or so to a ravine carpeted with rich green grass. It undulated down until it ended in a cliff above the Pacific Ocean. Along the sides of the green were a number of cabins and directly to the right of Edi's car was an old white inn with flower boxes on each window and a large deck overlooking the view of the ocean. Edi got out of the car and breathed in the slightly salty smell of the water. She wanted to get signed in so she could wander around the grounds before dinnertime.

"Welcome to Heritage House, Mrs. Harris. I see you are from Indiana. That's a long way away. How did you hear of Heritage House?" the woman registering Edi asked as she had a young man take her bag to the cabin she had been assigned.

"I read about you in a travel magazine. The pictures of the place were so beautiful, I made my mind up that one day I would come here. They said that the movie *Same Time Next Year* was filmed here and that the cabin facing the cove was the one used by Alan Alda. "Yes, that is true. We have a number of guests wanting to stay in that same cabin. When you walk around the grounds, you will pass it. Chris will take you to your cabin, if you are ready."

Edi followed the young man down a walk to a cabin on the right side of the green. Each cabin had been strategically built so they had unobstructed views of the green and the Pacific beyond. Edi unpacked and walked down the green, noticing people sitting on the decks in front of their cabins. It was approaching late afternoon, and the sun was beginning its descent. The breeze was cool, and the air smelled of pine trees in addition to the salty tang of the ocean. Edi walked down to the gazebo at the edge of the cliff. She sat down and looked out over the water. It was absolutely heavenly. She had never seen anything so magical.

When it was turning toward evening, Edi walked back to her cabin and picked up a sweater. She had reserved a table on the restaurant deck. They had thoughtfully lit their outdoor heater so it was quite comfortable outside. Edi found she was not eating alone. She was seated at a table with a couple from Illinois. They spent the meal comparing their home states and sharing a bottle of wine from the Napa Valley. They watched the sky turn from blue to gold as the sun set. It was a pleasant evening. Edi went back to her cabin, very satisfied with her first night at the Inn. As she settled down for the night, she could hear the distant sound of the ocean. It was so restful. Her last thought was how much Henry would have loved this place.

Chapter 16

Just as Edi was enjoying her stay in California, Elli and Stan were taking in the historic sites in London. So far, they had taken a ride on a double-decker bus, seen Westminster Abbey, and taken a walk through a part of Hyde Park. They had stopped for lunch at Fortnum & Mason's and did a bit of shopping at the legendary store. They toured the Tower of London that afternoon, and by evening, both Elli and Stan were toured out.

"We have to pace ourselves, or we will be too exhausted to enjoy anything. Tomorrow, let's just go to the Houses of Parliament, see Big Ben and Churchill's war rooms, and maybe walk a bit in Saint James's Park. How does that sound to you, Elli?" Stan asked as they sat in a pub where Stan was sampling a Guinness stout.

"I agree. There is just so much to see. I love walking the streets and just looking at everything. I do want to go to Harrods just to see the food stores on the main floor. I also want to see Buckingham Palace and—"

Stan stopped her from going on. "I have seen your list, dear. We'll do as much as we can, but I would like to spend at least one day going out of London to see the countryside, maybe take a train to Yorkshire. Now let's take one of these famous London taxi cabs back to the hotel and get ready for dinner."

As they drove back to Brown's Hotel, they couldn't help but notice the ethnic variety of people walking down the streets. Stan asked the driver if immigration had had a major impact on London. The driver responded saying that most of the immigrants were coming from the Middle East and were Muslims. "In my opinion, they are ruining the

London I grew up in, and we are having to support them. At my son's school, his teachers have to stop lessons so they can say their prayers. Just look at the women in their black outfits with their faces covered. They are all over," he replied.

Before they got out of the cab at their hotel, Stan said to the driver, "We are having some of the same problems in the States. Let's hope these issues resolve themselves."

* * *

It was the end of August. Stan and Elli regretfully left England. Edi watched her final sunset over the Pacific and drove back to San Francisco to catch her flight home. On the last Friday before September began, they gathered for martinis and to share pictures and souvenirs from their trips. They had invited the Websters and the Richters to join them and catch them up on what had gone on while they were away.

"You can put your mind at rest, Edi. I stopped by the museum a few times, and it was busy. Your docents were handling everything very well. There's not much else to report. Those political spots petered out. I guess they were not getting any positive feedback from the public. As you would expect, the weather has been hot and humid, and that's kept most of us indoors," said Opal. With no other news to discuss, they spent the rest of the evening talking more about England's sites and the California coast.

The next day, Stan met with his sons to see how his construction business had fared while he was away. Bobby told his father that they had fired one of the workmen who had been on the maintenance crew at the museum. He was the one who had been leaking information. Stan was glad to hear this. Everything else was going well. Stan knew he could leave anytime he wanted and his sons could run the business. He told both of them that he was going to semiretire and let them run the business and keep him posted on the daily operations. It was a good feeling to know that his sons could carry on Baxter Construction on their own.

* * *

Norm Mason at the Shell station, ripped August off his wall calendar and said to Lou, his gas station attendant, "We may be starting the fall, but it sure don't feel like it." The day was hot and humid with thunderclouds on the horizon. September wasn't off to a promising start.

"I wish it would rain, if it's going to," said Elli. "It just might break the heat and give us some cooler weather." A few moments later there was a clap of thunder and a flash of lightning.

"That's heat lightning," said Stan. "We are going to get some rain, but it probably won't cool things down. Once it is over, the heat will come back."

"Thank goodness for our pond and woods. They help keep us a bit cooler. But just look at me, I am perspiring, and I have only been outside on the patio for a few minutes," Elli exclaimed.

Stan looked up at the rainclouds and said, "Come on, we'd better get inside before the rain starts. This deluge shouldn't last long, but it has spoiled my golf game for today. The grounds will be too wet. This means I am all yours for the day. Any chores you need done?"

"As a matter of fact, there is something you can do. How about editing all the video footage we took in England and putting it together to show to our friends?" Elli said, smiling at Stan. And so they spent the better part of the first day of September making their home video of England.

As the rain cascaded off downspouts and awnings, people ran for cover. The Trellis Tea Room was packed with dripping customers. Museum visitors waited in the lobby for the rain to stop or slack off enough to get to their cars or buses. Edi, sitting at her desk, listened to the steady drumming of the rain on the roof.

"If this goes on much longer, we probably won't have too many visitors this afternoon," she said to one of the docents. They both stared out at the rain.

There was only one political media spot the first week of September. It was a self-serving one minute extolling the contribution Bexley made to the state of Indiana. When Stan casually asked people if they had seen it, most people didn't know what he was talking about. So much for politicians.

The first week of September passed slowly. Stan said he thought most families were getting ready for school and probably had forgotten about the upcoming *PBS Sunday Morning News Hour* and its Bexley feature. He called the Bexley paper and asked them to run a front-page article reminding everyone to watch the program Sunday morning. Edi was glad Stan had thought to do this because she realized that while it was top of mind for a few, it had probably dropped off the radar for most of the townspeople.

Edi, Elli, Opal, and Sandra had decided not to pursue any of the actions they had come up with during their strategic iced tea meeting. It all seemed pretty moot at this point. Stan and Elli invited everyone to their house to watch the Sunday morning broadcast over brunch. This would be a housewarming for their new home. Since the program was due to start at 9:00 a.m., Elli asked everyone to come at eight thirty so they could have their coffee or tea as they watched. They wanted to be ready when the program began since they didn't know at what time their feature would be shown. Stan was going to tape their feature so they could watch It again as they drank bloody marys and had their brunch.

There was a good article in the newspaper to help everyone remember to watch the Sunday morning program. The *Indianapolis Gazette* interviewed Edi and ran the interview in their Sunday paper. Indiana was going to get good press since people across the entire country would be viewing the PBS program.

Finally, Sunday morning arrived. It was sunny and mild, with a slight breeze blowing across the flowers and trees. Everyone had assembled at Elli and Stan's by 8:00 a.m. They got their coffee or tea and settled in for the viewing.

The program began with features on a famous artist and the drought in California. Then Charles Davis was introducing the audience to the small town of Bexley, Indiana, that, all on its own, had created a museum honoring the people who helped wage World War II from their home front. The cameras panned along the town and the museum. They saw Peggy Davis watering the flowers on Magazine Street and people spending a typical day visiting the stores and shops of their home town. When the camera took the audience into the museum, Charles paused so they could hear the music of the1940s playing softly. They were taken past the displays and exhibits that showed what the people of Bexley had done to support their fighting men and women. Charles showed how the mannequins added a sense of realism to each of the displays. As the camera panned up to the little theater, a one-minute clip of the 1940s film was shown. Then the camera paused to show the 1940 Ford up on blocks, still waiting for its owner to come home from the war. The feature ended with a view of the last display, with the minister celebrating the end of the war and the beginning of peace. Charles Davis came back in view saying there were home fronts all over America, but only here in Bexley had they taken the time and care to remind the country what patriotism is all about.

Everyone was moved. Elli was wiping her eyes, and Sam Richter had to clear his throat before he said, "That was excellent. I'll tell you, I am really proud to live in this town."

Stan turned and looked at Edi. He said, "Everyone should thank Edi for initiating and guiding the whole community to create the museum and make our town so important on the Indiana map. Our heartfelt thanks, Edi."

Edi shook her head. "I appreciate your kind words, but it took all of us to accomplish this. I may have gotten the ball rolling, but you all were integral in its success. Let's toast that."

Stan poured the bloody marys, and everyone raised their glass. Some hugs were exchanged, and they sat down to have their brunch. However, it wasn't a minute later that the phone rang. It was the first of dozens of calls from people all over the town, looking for Edi or Elli or Stan to tell them how terrific they thought the PBS show was. The editor of the *Bexley News* called and wanted to set up interviews for the next day. Sunday became a hectic day. Neighbors on Maple Drive came knocking on the door to say how much they had enjoyed the broadcast. When martini time came, it was an exhausted Stan, Elli, and Edi who sat on the back patio and reflected on how the day and the program had gone. Before they called it a night, Edi remarked that she was going to be glad when things got back to normal.

* * *

As the days passed and summer began to wane, the excitement over the television broadcast began to die down. Edi and Elli could walk down the streets of town without being stopped by neighbors congratulating them on the PBS show.

"You know, Elli, as Andy Warhol once said, I think we have had our fifteen minutes of fame," Edi commented.

Elli giggled. She said, "Aren't you glad it is over? I know I am. I want to enjoy my new home, spend time learning to play golf as Stan has asked me to, and do some volunteer work in the community."

Edi nodded, then added, "I want to concentrate on the museum, figuring out ways to ensure that it won't lose attendance and have to close. I am worried about this because, up till now, we have had the tourists and tour buses to guarantee a steady stream of visitors. But with the fall here, we will not be able to depend on them. I know we talked about hosting school tours, but that will not be enough to keep us out of the red. It would be a shame if after all this, the museum faded into obscurity."

"Edi, the community wouldn't allow this to happen," said Elli. "They have put too much effort into building it."

"Perhaps you are right. I will ask Opal and Sandra to sound out the town council and the mayor to see if they would be willing to help fund it on an ongoing basis. I had better put together a financial overview of museum costs so they will know what they are talking about," replied Edi.

A week later Mayor Haywood and the town council reviewed the financial projections prepared by Edi.

The mayor spoke first. "I had no idea running a museum involved so many expenses. I am assuming you have found the most cost-effective sources for maintenance, repairs, and upkeep."

"Yes, we have. I can assure you we have kept expenses to the minimum. As you can see, I am not taking any salary, and even the docents are all volunteers. So these costs are strictly to maintain and do upkeep on the museum and building itself," Edi replied.

The council spent several hours debating their role in funding the museum. Finally, after those supporting and those opposed finished their arguments, it was decided to table the issue for a month to see how the museum did on its own.

As Stan poured the evening martinis, he said, "I think they are putting off the inevitable. They don't want to be in a position where they are responsible for the success or failure of the museum. After all, the town will blame them if the enterprise closes. On the other hand, the costs for upkeep will have to come from other parts of the town's budget."

"You know, I feel partly responsible for this dilemma," said Edi. I never thought ahead when we got the museum started. If I had, I would have taken the time to think about the museum's future, and anticipated the financial impact on the community. But I didn't, and that is why we are in this situation now."

"Don't blame yourself, Edi. The town council and the whole community were involved from the beginning. Everyone was gung ho over it and I doubt if anyone thought about the loss of visitors and the effect of that on keeping the museum afloat," remarked Stan. "Let's give everything a month and see where we are then. We might be surprised and find visitors still making the trip from other parts of the state. Who knows?"

* * *

And so September drifted into October. The maple leaves were turning a rich red and gold against the blue fall sky. Children were kicking the fallen leaves as they came home from school. The weather was cool and breezy. Just right for trick or treating in a week when Halloween came to town. Already the first haystacks could be seen out past Bexley Acres. Pumpkins were growing out on the farms past Forsythe Field. Mothers had finished canning the summer fruit. For many, this was considered the best time of the year.

The lawns in Bexley were prepared for Halloween night. There were skeletons and scarecrows and even small tombstones adorning front yards. Here and there, people had pasted black cats and red devil masks on their windows. Most homes had a carved pumpkin with a candle shining inside. The pharmacy and the grocery had sold a lot of candy, which meant a good harvest for the kids trick-or-treating. It was the usual Halloween most towns looked forward to. Harold Kinsky, chief of police, had warned his men to be vigilant as they patrolled the neighborhoods. They didn't plan on arresting anyone, just making sure that no serious vandalism occurred.

They were keeping their eyes out for the Kelsey twins. Billy and Tommy were twelve going on twenty-five. They were a mischievous pair. Lately, their behavior had begun to turn dark. The police had found several dead cats in the woods at the end of Maple Drive. The poor things had been tied to trees and left to starve. The Kelsey twins had been seen in the area, but there was no evidence linking them to the cats' deaths. But because of this, the police were told to be on the lookout for them just in case they were up to more serious mischief. The two patrol cars drove slowly up and down the streets of Bexley, noting the kids in their costumes visiting the houses and gathering their candy. They would have been driving down the streets in any town in America and seen the same happy sights.

"The Chief said to keep an eye out for the Kelsey boys. He says he thinks they might do something serious because of what he thinks they did to those cats we found," Officer Dodd said.

At about eight thirty, Billy and Tommy emerged from their garage. They had filled an old soda bottle with gasoline and stuck a rag in the opening. Their plan was to throw it at a car driving down Maple Drive. They were going to start running as soon as it exploded.

"Why didn't we think of this for the Fourth of July?" Tommy asked Billy. "It would have been great to do as the fireworks were going on."

"Yeah. If this works real good, we can do at on the Fourth next year," Billy answered.

"I hate this town and all the snotty people in it," cried Tommy. "Why did Dad have to die and Mom have to work two jobs? Nobody cares about us. I know Mom used to care, but now all she does is go to work and sleep. I can't wait to get out of here."

Billy grabbed the bottle and said, "Come on, let's go."

As they ran up their street, they knocked over a child in a Batman suit and took his candy. The child's mother ran up and comforted her son. "Don't worry, sweetheart, I have more candy at home. Did those boys hurt you? Do you know who they are? I am going to call their mother when we get home," she said.

"Look over to your right. There are the Kelsey twins. Looks like they are up to something. Speed up and cut them off," said Officer Dodd.

The patrol car drove up over the curb and stopped. Both officers jumped out and grabbed the twins. The gasoline bottle was confiscated, and the boys were taken down to the police station. Their mother was called. When she arrived and heard what her sons were about to do, she cried.

With her hand covering her eyes, she said, "Since their father died, it's been so hard to look after them. I have to work two jobs, and when I get home, all I can do is sleep. I didn't know they were getting into trouble. They miss their dad. We don't have any other family, it is just me and the boys." She reached out and gathered both boys to her in a loving embrace. The boys were crying. It was a pretty emotional scene.

The police chief sat back at this desk, his arms folded and a serious expression on his face. He said, "You boys know what you were about to do could have killed someone. It is a punishable offence. I am not going to arrest you, but what I am going to do is sentence you to one hundred hours of community service working under Officer Pirofalo. He is a former Marine sergeant. You will report to him in this office tomorrow morning at nine o'clock. If you do not arrive on time, I will make the sentence two hundred hours. Are we clear?"

The boys and their mother said yes, and they took a tearful leave.

"If anyone can turn those boys around, it's Pirofalo. In future years, they will thank him for giving them pride, dignity, and self-respect. I sincerely hope this turns them in the right direction," he said.

* * *

Once Halloween was over, things calmed down. The weather turned colder; the wind became brisk. Elli was taking golf lessons from Coach Brown and found she really liked the game and the beauty of the course. Stan was patient and encouraging as they began to play together. The number of visitors to the museum tapered off, although the tour buses continued making it a stop for their Indiana tours, which helped boost attendance.

The town settled into pre-Thanksgiving mode. Shops and stores took down their Halloween displays. Some replaced them with cardboard turkeys while others skipped right to Christmas with Santa Claus, fake decorated trees and Christmas packages. Bexley was approaching the festive season. Where a few weeks ago you went to buy a pumpkin, you soon could go and look for a Christmas tree.

Thanksgiving meant families getting together for a huge meal and digesting it while watching football on TV. Stan and Elli were planning to have Edi and Stan's sons and their families over. This meant adding the extra leaves to the new dining table. It was going to be a wonderful family dinner. There would be wine with dinner, and later Stan would whip up a batch of martinis for those who wanted them. Already, Elli had set out a small corn stalk and a wreath of red berries on the front door.

Elli was in charge of turkey, potatoes, and vegetables, while Edi was preparing fruit cups, rolls, and dessert. Edi had prepared her pumpkin and mince pies and was working on her special fruit cup with coconuts and toasted walnuts. Elli was doing two turkeys, one with cornbread stuffing, the other with sausage stuffing. This was a meal with something for everyone. The dinner was set for two o'clock.

The family members started arriving, and Stan had his sons and the children outside playing with Frisbees. Edi and Elli were busy getting the food into serving dishes and platters.

When everything was ready, Elli brought in the first turkey for Stan to carve. Everyone sat down, and Edi lighted the candles gracing the table. It was a lovely scene. In fact, it looked like a Norman Rockwell painting.

Once everyone was seated, Elli asked them to take each other's hands for a Thanksgiving tribute. "As we go around the table, would each of you say what you are thankful for? I will begin." Looking at Stan, she said, "I am thankful to be married to such a wonderful, loving man. He has given me true happiness."

Next came Edi. She smiled and said, "I am thankful for being asked to help unite our community and create such a special museum—oh, and for my beautiful new home!"

One by one, Stan's sons and their wives expressed their gratitude for something they had either achieved or been given during the year.

When it finally came back around the table to Stan, he looked at Elli and his family and said, "I am thankful I have all of you, and especially that I found this woman who makes my life complete. I love you, my dear." As he said this, Stan raised his wineglass and said, "Let's raise our glasses and ask God to bless this family." Stan looked over at the children's table and asked what they were thankful for.

Little Pete chirped up, "Grandpa, I will be thankful if you give me a big drumstick!"

On that note, with lots of laughter, the family began their Thanksgiving feast.

After dinner, as always happens, the women cleared the table and did the dishes, the men watched football and talked about the construction business. This was a scene replicated in homes all over America. Yet Bexley was unique in one way, because of its home front museum it honored all the home fronts in America.

Epilogue

It was autumn in Bexley, Indiana. Three years had gone by since the museum had been built. Someone familiar with the town would notice the changes that had occurred. On the surface, the town had grown. The road coming in from Bloomington now had a modest hotel called the Home Front Hotel. Going down Magazine Street, in addition to the older shops and stores, some new ones had been added. There was the Catered Affair, a shop that did special cakes and desserts as well as catering for special events. A few steps down was Laurie's Fashion Boutique, offering one-of-a-kind outfits and jewelry. At the end of the main block, the old Ace Hardware had been torn down and replaced by an Outdoor Outfitters store. It sold everything from hunting and fishing gear to outdoor clothing. It had grown very popular with local townspeople and with the people in Bexley's Acres. Reverend Wilson's Universal Baptist Church had a new addition.

At a quick glance, everything else seemed pretty much the same. But some changes were not so visible. The Kelsey boys were doing well. Billy was a star in basketball, and Tommy was planning on joining the Marines when he graduated. Peggy Davis, with support from her uncle Charles, was a sophomore at Indiana State, majoring in economics. Mayor Haywood had retired and been replaced by Whitney Hall, a young man eager to "bring Bexley up-to-date." Outside of town, a technology company had erected a large facility and hired a number of Bexley people. It was talking about adding another plant, and this would mean more new hires.

Forsythe Field had been enlarged so it could handle larger airplanes made necessary by the tech company. On the road to Bloomington, there was now a Walmart, and it had hired quite a few people from Bexley. As the businesses grew, the population increased. Not only did the town profit from this, so did Bexley Acres, where some of the new people bought lots and built new homes. This caused the grocery and drug store to add second stores in the area. This new focus also brought in a pizza parlor, a secondhand store, a barber shop, and a beauty parlor. All of this caused the price of homes in Bexley Acres to increase in value. Bexley Acres now sported more new cars, dish satellites and additions to homes, and less farmyard animals.

Stan had turned over the business entirely to his sons. He and Elli were devoting their time to the grandchildren and to taking trips to places that took their fancy. Just this year, they had been to Venice and Acapulco.

Edi was kept busy in the museum. She no longer had to worry about the museum closing down because of declining attendance. It was now owned by the State of Indiana, which meant it was fully funded. Another plus was that the politicians had stopped wrangling over it. Being a state museum meant a good stream of visitors throughout the year.

A sign had been erected on both sides of the road leading into town. It said. "You are entering Bexley, Indiana, a town known for its Home Front Museum. Stop and visit—you will be glad you did."

CPSIA information can be obtained
at www.ICGtesting.com
Printed in the USA
FFOW03n0526190917
40107FF

9 781543 446104